Leicester Writes

Short Story Prize 2020

First published 2020 by Dahlia Publishing Ltd
6 Samphire Close Hamilton
Leicester LE5 1RW
ISBN 9781913624026

Selection copyright © Dahlia Publishing 2020

Copyright of each piece lies with individual authors © 2020

The moral right of the authors has been asserted.

All rights reserved. No part of this publication may be reproduced, stored in or introduced into a retrieval system, or transmitted, in any form, or by any means (electronic, mechanical, photocopying, recording or otherwise) without the prior written permission of the publisher. Any person who does any unauthorized act in relation to this publication may be liable to criminal prosecution and civil claims for damages.

Printed and bound by Grosvenor Group

This book is sold subject to the condition that it shall not, by way of trade or otherwise, be lent, re-sold, hired out, or otherwise circulated without the publisher's prior consent in any form of binding or cover other than that in which it is published and without a similar condition including this condition being imposed on the subsequent purchaser.

A CIP catalogue record for this book is
available from The British Library

CONTENTS

Foreword • Farhana Shaikh

Dissolution • Dan Powell	1
The Taste of Sugar • Joe Bedford	9
Not Entirely True • Alison Woodhouse	20
Swimming Against the Tide • Claire Sheret	28
The Reddifers • Peter Hankins	40
Required Reading • Laura Blake	51
Packing like a Brownie Guide • Judith Wilson	64
Faith • Fiona Ennis	74
Sarika and Me • Radhika Praveen	83
Steel Hearts • Harjit Keanu Singh	95
Bottled Up • Matt Kendrick	104
The Naughty Step • Maureen Cullen	112

Velocity • Farhana Khalique	119
Pancake Day • Judy Birkbeck	125
The Curd Maker • Tania Brassey	136
Mooly • J. R. McMenemie	145
Black and White Blues • Richard Hooton	153
Continental Breakfast • Ed Barnfield	166
The Queue • Miki Lentin	177
Washing Day • Katherine Hetzel	185
About the Authors	*195*
Judging Panel	*203*

THE LEICESTER WRITES SHORT STORY PRIZE 2020

Foreword

The Leicester Writes Short Story Prize was set up to celebrate the short story form and to showcase the very best new writing. So it's a real honour to present this anthology which features twenty exceptional stories longlisted in this year's competition.

In our fourth year, we received just over 160 entries from across the country and the overall quality was outstanding. It's always a fascinating exercise to see what themes and topics writers are exploring in their work but what writers were preoccupied with during this strange and unprecedented time was especially revealing. Some stories were, of course, inspired by Covid 19 itself bringing our new reality into sharp focus. There were stories which were filled with nostalgia, which played with style or disguised themselves in other forms. There were plenty of stories inspired by sex and romance which in itself probably told us more than we cared to know.

Each submission was read by our filter judges before the highest scoring entries were sent to our judging panel, chaired by Rebecca Burns, our 2018 winner Selma Carvalho and Leicester-based writer Mark Newman. They read each of the stories separately before coming together to share and deliberate over the shortlist and our worthy winners. I'd like to thank them for the care and attention they took in arriving at what must have been an incredibly difficult decision

The stories placed in the top four are pitch perfect and do what successful short stories must do – draw us into their world and keep us reading until the final sentence.

Our highly commended story, 'Swimming Against the Tide' by Claire Sheret is beautifully observed and a wonderful lesson in characterisation. I couldn't quite believe that it's Claire's first ever submission to a short story competition! In third place 'Not Entirely True' by Alison Woodhouse pulls us into the childhood memories of an unnamed protagonist as she recalls the details of a life-changing accident. Our runner-up, 'The Taste of Sugar' by Joe Bedford, is a masterclass in using the senses to create mood and help readers think and feel. And finally our winning story, 'Dissolution' by Dan Powell, is a poignant tale told with precision.

I hope you enjoy the short stories in this collection and discover a favourite among them.

THE LEICESTER WRITES SHORT STORY PRIZE 2020

Dissolution
DAN POWELL

It was shortly after Dad left that last time that Mum took to painting on the flat roof of the house. You might not remember, but we arrived home from school to find her up there, her easel nailed through the EPDM rubber to the thick roof timbers beneath. Fixed upon the easel, a half-completed watercolour of the horizon ruffled lightly in the breeze.

I tried to talk her down, but she refused. She had set up our old pop-up tent and fixed it there and planned to stay right there on the roof, she said, painting until she got the sky right. So, with rope from the shed, I secured the ladder she had left propped against the house and brought her meals up to her in Tupperware boxes.

We waited for her to complete her painting but however many times she began, she always grew dissatisfied with the image before her, removed it and pinned it to the rubber roof covering with large brass drawing pins. Within a week she had covered the roof with these unfinished images. When the breeze picked up the edges of her half-painted skylines, they fluttered and flickered against each other in a haunting paper murmuration.

All through those first days she was up there, after I had put the two of you to bed, I sat with her on the roof through the late spring evenings. Wrapped in my school coat, I watched her paint. I hoped perhaps, as the sky darkened and night set in, to convince her to climb down with me and return to the house, but she never did. So I walked you to school each day before heading in to college myself, then raced back at the end of the day to collect you. I prepared your meals, I bathed you both, I read to you both and I put you to bed, and in between I climbed back and forth to the roof to check on Mum and deliver her meals, her bottles of water and flasks of tea, her clean clothes, her new paints and art paper.

You have both asked why I did these things, why I didn't refuse, why I enabled her, but you are probably too young to even remember the other times Dad left. Probably too young to remember the time she shut herself away in the dining room and papered the walls with anatomical sketches of a male body that I think now must have been Dad's, or the time she locked herself in the garage and constructed sculptures from the car parts and tools and all the other crap Dad had left behind there. She did these things as if the doing of them might summon him back. And you probably don't remember how those obsessions faded and she slipped back to us, even before Dad turned up back on the doorstep, a day or so later, with his stupid sorry grin and his bag full of dirty washing. I thought this was simply just another one of those times. I was wrong.

As the days passed and the pinned, half-finished paintings spread across the rooftop, I asked her what it was exactly she was trying to capture.

I will know it when I have it, she said.

She did not look at me as she spoke, just kept her eyes fixed on the image on her easel and the skyline beyond. It was for the most part thick with cloud, a wash of greyscale formations, tinged a fiery orange at the western horizon. I sat with her and watched the shifting form and colour of it. The sound of my breath and the gentle clattering of my mother's brush as she cleaned it against the easel were the only sounds.

Sitting there, watching the sky and watching her work, I forgot the need to persuade her to come inside. As she painted, I waited for a glimpse of what it was she was searching for, but I saw only shifting cloud and light. I saw only an image eternally unfolding, impossible to capture.

The rain held off that first week she spent up there. The pinned, unfinished paintings multiplied, the paint and paper drying in the sun. The noise of them, ruffling and snapping in the breeze, grew until finally the rain came. I was in the kitchen when the downpour began and, grabbing my coat, I raced outside and up the ladder. Mum was sat at her easel, still working, even as the rain washed the colours of her painting into a murky grey.

Mum, you must come down now, it isn't safe to be up here, I said as I reached her. She didn't look at me, only shook her head.

I must finish this, she said.

She dabbed at the painting with her brush, but I could see the image was lost. When I took Mum's arm and tried to guide her up from her seat, she finally turned and looked at me.

What are you doing? she said.

I didn't answer. For a moment, in the shadow of the black clouds rolling above us, her face itself was a blur. Streaks of paint, grey and green and black, spread down her cheeks from the dark bags under her eyes. The rain was washing her face away along with the image on the easel before her.

Leave me be, she said and raised a hand to wave me away.

Her hands were streaked with colour, and as the rain spattered upon them, diluted paint dripped from the ends of her fingers. But more than that, her fingers seemed to shorten as the colour washed from them, as if she herself were dissolving.

I dragged her from her chair then and away from her easel, bundled us both into the shelter of the tent. I sat across the entrance, blocking her exit, and I turned on the small camping light she kept there. She sat silently, staring past me to the easel outside as I wiped the smears of paint from her face and hands with an old tea towel until she was once more herself and I was left feeling embarrassed at the ridiculousness of my own imaginings.

The rain poured for hours. Mum just sat in the tent, her palette beside her, her large water colour pad upon her lap. There she painted the shifting greys and blacks, the hints of distant blue, while all across the roof the rain hammered her then, up at the roof. Mum was stood there, by the ladder, looking down at us both. For a moment I thought she was about to climb down, but she just stood there. She had her brush in her hand and slowly she raised it in front of her and pointed down at Dad. She held the brush horizontally between thumb and forefinger in that way she did when measuring the depth or breadth of something. She did not move for a moment and I said to Dad again, Please just talk to her. Again he shook his head. No, he said finally, I'm sorry, I just can't. I wondered if Mum could hear him, but when I looked to the roof, she had moved from the ladder, had gone back to her painting. Before he drove away, Dad rolled down his window, and called me over. Look after your brother and sister, he said, and ring me if things get worse. I nodded and said I would, but I knew I wouldn't ring him, knew there would be no point.

That night the rains came again. The roof itself was once more covered with incomplete images of the skyline, each one fixed in place with bright brass pins. I was curled on the sofa in a deep sleep, having planned to only settle there for a moment after putting the two of you to bed. I didn't hear the rain, though it must have thundered on the windows. I slept right through, only waking early the next morning.

The house was quiet. You two were still asleep and so I rushed to get my trainers and my coat. Outside, the air had that washed, clear quality that comes after a heavy rainfall. I called to Mum as I climbed the ladder. She didn't reply.

unfinished works. The downpour dissolved the paint upon the paper, making abstract streaks and spatters and smudges of colour out of the half-defined skylines.

By the time the sun came out most of the paintings had been pulped to a grey sludge. Only fragments remained fixed to the brass pins, scraps of smeared colour that looked nothing like the sky. I watched as my mother stepped from the tent into the bright sun. She said nothing as she circled the roof, putting a hand to a few of the remaining fragments, tracing her fingers through the smeared mess of colours there, coating her fingertips with dank shades. Then she reset her easel without saying a word and sat and stared deep into the fresh sheet of paper pinned there. It was as if some image were already visible to her within its emptiness.

A week or so later, Dad came home. You were both in school that day, but I had a study day and was at home keeping an eye on Mum. This time he didn't knock and there was no silly grin or bag of washing. Instead he pulled up outside in a rusty Transit van, threw open the rear doors and dragged a handful of empty cardboard boxes from inside.

Can't you at least just talk to her? I said to Dad as he packed his things. He just shook his head and continued emptying his wardrobe into suitcases I had not seen since we stopped going on family holidays. I asked him again as he loaded up the van, but he just shook his head and slammed the van doors closed. He looked back to the house

THE LEICESTER WRITES SHORT STORY PRIZE 2020

The rain had pulped every one of the paintings pinned to the roof. Their sludged remains blotched the roof's rubber membrane in a mess of grey. The paper pinned to the easel was the only one that remained remotely intact and even that was ruined. The force of the rain had torn the paper itself in places; gouges like claw marks slashed the abstracted image that remained.

At first, I thought Mum must be in the tent, but, as I neared, its unzipped flaps fluttered open to reveal her empty sleeping bag. I looked about the roof, ran to its edges and peered down along each side of the house, half-certain I would find her heaped on the ground below, but I found no sign of her anywhere.

It was as I walked back toward her easel that I noticed the dark shape smeared across her chair and the puddle of colour pooled beneath it. Looking closer, crouching beside the chair, I could see the colours, could even hear the colours, mixed almost to a perfect black, as they drip-drip-dripped from the seat of the chair down onto the rubber roof covering. I watched the paint puddle swell and spread, struggling to understand, but the puddle remained shapelessness and indecipherable.

Stood there, beside all that remained of her, I looked away, out past the easel. The sky seemed suddenly frozen, the bright blue of its expanse tinged grey and white where the few remaining clouds hung unmoving. I stared deep into its breadth, its height for I don't know how long, half expecting to find whatever it was she had been looking for suddenly revealed, but there was nothing but empty sky spreading out above me, and I might have stood there searching forever if one of you hadn't called my name from where you stood on the front step in your pyjamas, hadn't asked me again, When is Daddy coming home?

THE LEICESTER WRITES SHORT STORY PRIZE 2020

The Taste of Sugar
JOE BEDFORD

Hôtel le Bristol, Paris

One by one I take the papers from my briefcase and stack them on the table: hotel reservations, train tickets, itineraries for the week. A waiter arrives and makes room for my madeleines. As he sets down the plate I find the clipping and hold it up to my eyes.

The obituary reminds me of a recipe. The details of her life are there – her birth, her work, her illness – but the flavour is absent.

I eat the madeleine with my eyes closed and try to remember.

Our newspaper dispatched us to Paris on the same ferry – me to cover the restaurant at le Bristol, Milena to cover de Gaulle's resignation. She'd been on Fleet Street for less than a year and had been proposed to twelve times. On the ferry, she sat at the bar reading Dorothy Parker for the duration. I walked the deck and ate bonbons.

We dined at le Bristol. During starters, she was guarded. During mains, aloof. Then came the madeleines.

A crisp scallop-shell skin, soft sponge wet and dense with butter. A fine film of vanilla floating on orange blossom water. Simple and perfect – those squat, plump little cakes.

Milena was transformed. The sweetness provoked her into something like epiphany. Her guard crumbled. As the first yellow flakes fell onto her plate, the details of her life spilt out.

She was born in Prague during the War. Her father had been a baker who was executed by the Germans. She worked for a journal I'd never heard of, specialising in the shortcomings of the Communists. She spoke with fire about the growing dissent, the rising backlash. She'd composed pamphlets during the Prague Spring. She even appeared on television. This, she admitted, was a mistake. That summer, Soviet tanks entered the country and took control without a fuss. She hung a road sign that read 'Moscow: 3200 kilometres' and fled.

She spoke candidly, wittily and with utter sincerity. By the time she'd finished talking and both our plates were clean, I was in love with her. We spent the night together, and two days later returned to London. It was as if I'd tasted life for the first time.

A waiter knocks over my cane, bends muttering to retrieve it, and removes my plate. The madeleines are not as sweet as I remember, though I know my sense of taste is waning.

The initial panic of beginning to lose my palette has faded. Like my memory, my hearing and my eyesight, it is a mark of decay that cannot be fought, only supplemented.

I rise with a grunt. I can remember the departure times of every train I'll take in the next five days, but standing here now, looking absently at the Christmas tree in the corner, I struggle to remember the sound of Milena's voice.

Bar Pompi, Rome

The express from Milan was full today, the streets of Rome crowded. My jacket, hung behind me on the chair, is wet with rain. The sound of Italians comparing newly-bought gifts fills Bar Pompi.

My tiramisu is boozy and compelling. The slap of the coffee is bold enough to evoke my memory, though at first only with disparate detail: Milena's face crinkled in mute pleasure; the unusual shape of a spoon that pleased her; the anxiety of waiting for an answer. But what had been the question?

With a rush of sugar from the tiramisu, the pieces begin to join back together.

The re-launched Pompi felt as fresh as ever, but there was an air of unease in the city after Prime Minister Moro's abduction. Milena wanted to interview members of the Red Brigade and that left me worried. So we ate quietly, until dessert was over.

Our love affair had coasted for ten years – the happiest of my life. We travelled regularly, following each other on assignments, holidaying throughout Europe. Milena was still unable to visit Prague, a fact she repeated at every airport. We were still young, but by then I was Food Editor and she a senior political correspondent. Offers of editorial positions came to her from all across the continent, but she remained in London. I told myself this was because of me, though she never indicated as much.

Our love was simple – physical and fun. Her total lack of sentimentality kept us grounded and our joy together kept things lively. We never once discussed taking a flat or getting married, nor did we ask about other lovers, though neither of us wanted them. We worked and travelled and ate, and that was all. It was a state of bliss.

When the bill came at Pompi, I broke the silence. As soon as the words came out, I regretted them.

'Do you think we should commit?'

She laughed. I think she took it for a misshapen proposal. She took my hand from across the table and we spoke uncharacteristically about love. She told me frankly and kindly that if we were married, our time together would become like food cooked at home, eaten daily on the same crockery, even away from the table, on trays on our laps.

I understood and agreed. But suddenly I didn't want my coffee. It was as if I'd accidentally dropped a spoon of salt into it.

My review of the re-launched Pompi was not as generous as it should've been. If I could write about it now, I'd call it a 'a sweet mascarpone dawn' – or at least something suggesting a glow. But maybe that is sentiment. In truth, even the flavour of the coffee is struggling to break through the ambiguity that is spreading over my tongue.

All flavours are dimming – their vivacity is slowly dying. And my memories of Milena are receding, even despite this final trip.

People are waiting to be seated. I've lingered here too long.

Café Sacher Wien, Vienna

Why did we come here, and when? I know we ate Sachertorte, and the sight of it arriving at my table for some reason evokes the word '*fröhliche*' – merry. I take a bite anxiously. The chocolate tastes flat and black. My eye catches the window. There had been a paper snowflake hanging there, so it must have been December, same as now. We were carrying heavy woollen coats we'd bought that day in Vienna. We drank schnapps, possibly.

I run my tongue across my dentures. Even though I can now remember why we were here I can't recall the year. I have a sudden urge to tug the waiter's sleeve, but I know he can't help me. What would I even ask him? When I was last here, he wouldn't have been born.

I'd followed Milena to Vienna because of a national disaster – something violent. She described the details to me as we ate. She'd seen blood that day. It was the airport attack at Schwechat – '85 or '86 – where tourists had been killed at an El Al check-in counter. She was agitated, since she'd been struggling to stay sympathetic to the PLO. Evidently, this was not all.

An Austrian couple at another table were laughing egregiously. It was the wrong time for me to praise the Sachertorte.

She lowered her fork – always an ominous signal – and spoke evenly. Something along the lines of: 'Have you listened to a word I've said?'

I had listened but I bungled relaying the number of casualties. She accused me of caring more about food than people.

'That's not true,' I said. 'I care about you immensely.'

That was not what she meant. Suddenly the conversation had nothing to do with Yasser Arafat or the Café Sacher but turned personal and explicit and ugly. I admitted no lack of conscience, even if I was not as political as she was. She speculated that I had no real interest in her work, except in the fact that it was hers and I felt I should 'keep my hand in'. I told her sharply that it didn't matter either way, which bothered her even more. She questioned whether we'd wasted those past fifteen years pretending to be gourmets, while writers were being jailed in Prague. At the word 'Prague' she burst into quiet, firm sobs which she immediately gathered up. She let me hold her hand but by then her mind was elsewhere.

The tortes, unfinished between us, appeared gluttonous, even gloating.

The apologies we made to each other were sincere but incomplete. I avoided Vienna completely after that, and haven't returned until today. It's painful to be here, in the same room we argued, but the pain is distant and abstracted. It belongs, like all the painful events of Europe in my lifetime, to the past.

I shiver. I'm thinking of tomorrow and the journey I have to make, and whether I'm able to bring myself to make it. There is only one more city I need to see to complete my memory of Milena, so I must make it. I must force myself.

Looking up, I see the café is closing. As I rise, the faint flavour of the Sachertorte has already become muddled. The paper snowflake is gone from the window.

Wenceslas Square, Prague

Wenceslas Square is covered in tourists – a disorienting blur of foreign languages and flash photography. I navigate by the Christmas lights above, past the Hotel Evropa, and search the vendors for *trdelnik*. I watch the rings of sugared dough spin rapidly over the coal, their surface a darkening crystal. I escape with one into a cobbled street and bite down into it. It tastes of nothing, a bready nothing, so I hold the crust on my tongue. My mouth waters to it. After a moment I taste the vague flavour of sugar.

Milena had called them 'chimney cakes' and she almost cried when she ate one. The streets were full that day too, not with tourists but with Prazaks of all generations holding banners, singing songs and sharing food. For weeks they'd been gathering and marching and preparing themselves for freedom. When Milena had seen the footage of students being beaten she packed a bag. She wanted to go alone but I insisted on following. I told her I wanted to protect her, but that wasn't the reason and neither of us believed it.

Pacing the square, drinking in the sense of change, she came alive. She spoke Czech ecstatically, with everyone, as if gorging after a prolonged hunger. She found someone she knew near the National Museum – a journalist of about her age who threw his arms around her. She laughed constantly, with flakes of *trdelnik* snowing down her coat. After a few hours, we sat down together at the foot of the statue.

I already sensed in myself that some great period of waiting had come to an end in both of us. So I was not surprised when she said: 'I'm staying.' I had predicted it, of course, long before we came. I told her that she looked, unquestionably, like she belonged. The Communists would be out within a week, and if Havel took office her reputation would get her an executive position at any paper. I was only surprised when she suggested I join her.

'I want you with me.'

It was the only statement of commitment she ever made. But it was too late. I had a life and a career in London. I had friends, family and a house. I was in my forties but still desperate to travel. And I was angry at the ease with which she decided to stay. So I refused.

She accepted it, predicted it also, I think. She knew when we arrived in Prague that I'd be leaving her behind. It was an inevitability I'd tried to prepare myself for. I'd failed.

We parted three days later, in the square.

I suck down on the *trdelník* and try to remember that moment.

We stood opposite each other holding hands – of that I'm sure. She was smiling, I think, and the band was playing some song I knew. I chew the *trdelník* and picture her lips moving. I see her speaking and chew, chew and try to hear the words. The crowded pieces of my memory are tumbling around like the cake inside my mouth. I reach out for her final parting words – the last words I heard her say – and try to taste. But I can't. I can't taste a thing, not even the sweetness of the sugar. Not even in the faintest way.

I walk away into the crowd and the words are lost.

Hôtel le Bristol, Paris

I'm back at le Bristol with a madeleine in front of me. The Eurostar leaves in an hour, so this will be my last bite to eat on the continent. I let it linger there untouched and only eventually tuck my napkin into my collar.

I've been retired for several years now, and every Christmas I receive phone calls from people who assume I'm alone. Most Christmas Days I'm found with friends, spooning out bland, slippery gobs of trifle, talking about

Fleet Street in the 1960s. This year I'll be with an editor, who'll boast about his children's book deals and his grandchildren's exam results. I'll tell him where I've been on my trip, though nothing of the reasons why. Then I'll go home to my beautiful house and read my Christmas cards, and write down whatever memories I can retrieve.

Food was my vocation, but now it is simply functional. Porridge takes me through the morning. Tea warms me when I'm cold. The real joy of it, even whilst my palette was relatively sharp, is long gone. As I take a bite of the madeleine, the taste is absent – only the contradictory textures give me pleasure. But, despite everything, the object still has the power to please, like a small, inexpensive work of art.

When I'm finished, I take out the obituary and place it on the empty plate.

There is nothing in it about the way Milena held her knife and fork, nothing about her face, over-pursed as she chewed. There is nothing about the way she spoke – the changes in her speech when she discussed food, politics, love. There is no indication of her courage, her stubbornness, her patriotism, her ability to listen, her inexplicably-charged hatred for boiled eggs, the missing incisor she never explained. There is nothing here of the real Milena, only a recipe.

Born: Prague, 1943. Died: Prague, 2018.

I pay the bill. A waiter helps me to the door and then into a taxi. I'll be home within three hours or so.

I leave dutifully, purposefully, wondering if I'm ready.

I leave only one thing behind with the obituary on the table, something I must be prepared to let go. It is my memory of the taste of sugar.

THE LEICESTER WRITES SHORT STORY PRIZE 2020

Not Entirely True
ALISON WOODHOUSE

When I was young, we had a long, thin garden that sloped up to the field behind the house. Just over the fence were two horse chestnuts and on either side of the path was a border of roses; the old fashioned, sweet-smelling, blowsy sort.

That's how I remember it but Mum never believed me. She would point at the photographs around the house and say they were my so-called memories and I should be careful not to trust what I thought I might know.

The summer I turned seven, Mum hired contractors and our garden became a car park for our white van with the disabled sticker. That autumn I listened to conkers fall onto tarmac, pit, pit, pit, whilst I sat at my desk copying sketches of pixies and elves into my art book. I watched Mum steer Dad in the wheelchair around the tarmac. She was always very erect. I didn't hear her talk to him. They just walked and wheeled, round and round. I didn't talk to him much either. When he tried to speak his mouth twisted into strange shapes, as if he was eating his own words. His speech therapist said he should improve, with patience and practice, and encouraged me to spend time with him but he frightened me.

Nobody told me about the accident but I've read all the newspaper reports: the drive home from the pub, the collision with a tree and Dad left with 'life changing' injuries. They didn't lock him up. The judge was lenient, said he'd already paid the ultimate penalty and as no one else was involved he didn't see any point in prison. The only mention I ever get is 'the child was unharmed'. This is not entirely true. I remember Mum shouting at me to get into the back seat while she carried on her argument with Dad outside the car, the tussle over the keys. I remember them still arguing whilst the engine revved. The noise of the impact. Being pulled out of my seat, the strap scraping my neck, the heat of the explosion. I woke up in hospital and lots of adults wanted to talk to me but I didn't say a word. They called it selective mutism, said I might have nightmares and need therapy, but Mum disagreed and when I showed no obvious signs of trauma the social workers stopped visiting and I suppose my file was closed.

A few years later, Mum decided it was time for me to walk to school on my own. It was less than a mile along a busy well-lit main road.

'Be a good girl and don't make a fuss,' she said. 'You've got to learn to stand on your own two feet and I don't always want you under mine.'

The street was different with nobody at my side. I stayed close to the wall, avoided cracks in the pavement and held my school bag in front of me, both arms around it. I felt exposed out there. Sometimes older children from school would swarm past, jostling me, once even trying to grab my bag but I'd hang on, curled around it. The children were louder and bigger and more carefree in the streets but I was exactly the same wherever I went.

Every Saturday, a carer came to be with Dad so Mum could go out. If she was meeting her sister, Aunt Linda, she dressed up in her blue outfit, a straight knee length skirt and a jacket with large brass buttons. She looked tight and smart and couldn't bend down. There was a white dressing table in her bedroom with a mirror and a stool and she laid out her make up before showering. Afterwards the bathroom would be full of steam and I'd go in there, shut the door and feel it coat my face like a mask. I'd write words on the mirror, words I heard other children shout and sing when they ran past me *spastic, fuckwit, cunt*. They disappeared like magic when I opened the window.

The regular carer was a lady called Susan who sat in Dad's room the whole time Mum was gone and did a crossword puzzle. She'd chat and didn't get angry or click her tongue against the back of her teeth when he never replied. Over time I learnt to sit in his room when Susan was there. I still didn't like looking at his mouth, his tongue half out and his jaw always moving. Susan dabbed his lips with moisturiser and mopped his cheeks when his eyes leaked. She told me to show him my drawings and when I did, he made noises that sounded like a turkey gobbling but Susan said he was happy and after that I started to go into his room even when she wasn't there.

One Saturday, another lady came. She had a handbag with a clasp that closed with a loud snap and seemed to know Mum quite well. They sat in the kitchen drinking coffee and I heard her say it was about time, but she stopped talking when I went in and asked for a glass of water.

The other lady didn't sit with Dad but stayed in the kitchen, smoking. Every time she got her out cigarettes I heard the snap, snap, snap of her bag.

I went to the library. I liked to tidy the shelves and replace the books other children left scattered on the floors. There were two old women who never bothered me except to ask if I wanted to join them in the office for orange juice or a biscuit. I always said no. If I was quiet enough they forgot I was there and I could slide a book into my satchel and take it home. I always returned it. I liked stealing, but it was far too easy.

I worked hard in school and did well. My reports said I was quiet and good. I've thought many times since how different those two things really are.

Mum spent most of her time reading. When she read, she pulled the standard lamp close so that it peered over her shoulder, lighting up the page, and she perched her glasses on the end of her nose, holding her book at arm's length, her chin tilted so that the lamplight cast deep shadows along the sides of her nose. The books came from the same library I used although we were never there at the same time. She took six books out on a Tuesday and another six on a Friday.

Romance. History. Thrillers. If I tried to talk to her when she was reading she'd swat the air. If I asked what she was reading, she grunted. I can still see her, bathed in a halo of light, her arms up, palms out, pushing me into the world, away from her.

I'd forage for supper, tins usually, as she wasn't interested in eating. She never had been. She developed intolerances that I now realise were almost certainly psychological. Headaches if she ate cheese, tummy upsets if she tried lentils. She did have a serious peanut allergy, though, and since the accident I'd been taught to use the EpiPen, just in case.

I was sixteen when Mum died. The secretary took me out of French and to the headmaster's office. I was used to the office: it was where he liked to hand out commendation certificates. There were two leather armchairs and I was invited to sit in one. The secretary arranged for a taxi to take me home. Aunt Linda was with Dad. I hadn't seen her for a very long time, but they were both crying, she noisily, he with swallowed grunts.

Aunt Linda sent me off to stay with my grandparents. They were perfectly kind, just old and bewildered. I stayed out of their way as much as possible, revising for my GCSE's until Aunt Linda came to take me home.

She was excited. She'd arranged for a lawyer to represent Dad at a compensation hearing and was very hopeful. She said it was time to claim for eleven years spent in a wheelchair, because of faulty brakes. Mum had always been adamant that she didn't want to drag everyone through all the sordid details but Aunt Linda wanted the garage, where the car had had its MOT, to pay.

'It wasn't brakes,' I said. 'The accident was Mum's fault.'

Aunt Linda shook her head but what did she know? She hadn't been there that day, hadn't heard the argument or seen Mum grab the keys from Dad and get into the driver's seat.

'You can't possibly remember all that. You were a child!'

She didn't believe me when I told her I still smell roses in my sleep as well.

The night before Mum died I was doing my homework at the kitchen table, eating tuna sweetcorn with mayonnaise. Her nose wrinkled.

'Couldn't you take that to your room?'

'Why don't you have some? You haven't eaten anything tonight.' She'd had plenty to drink though. A whole bottle gone and another already open.

'Why don't you go and sit with your dad?'

'I want to sit with you.'

'I don't need your company. He's the one who's lonely.'

'He's okay. Countdown is on.'

'You don't understand. You don't remember him before the accident.' Mum started crying in that way drunk people do, one eye on their audience. I knew the routine but I didn't want her talking about it again, what it had been like before

I was born, how happy they'd been, how wrong it had all gone. I was supposed to comfort her, that was my job, but instead I left her slumped on the table and did what she'd told me. I sat on the floor next to Dad's chair watching the television, eating a packet of dry roasted peanuts I'd shoplifted on the way home from school. I heard the grunts he made, saw his eyes flash between the peanuts and me and back again, his agitated swallows, because they were, of course, not allowed in our house.

Before I went upstairs I laid up our breakfast, as usual. Toast plate and milk glass for me, Dad's tray with a bowl for his gloopy porridge and a carton of juice and a coffee cup for Mum, which was all she'd ever have in the morning. I ground down a quarter of a peanut in the pestle and mortar and stirred the dust into the inch of coffee left at the bottom of the jar. When I went to bed I stopped outside her room. She'd fallen asleep reading, her mouth slightly open, her glasses down her nose. She looked very peaceful.

It's ten years since she died. With the money the lawyers got from the out of court settlement, we've opened up the house. Downstairs is a large living room with an adapted kitchen, a corner sofa, a huge television on the wall and a music system and Dad's bedroom has French windows. We've got a garden again too, a lawn and a path lined with roses, the old fashioned, sweet-smelling, blowsy sort.

Dad is smaller these days, sunk into the seat of his chair, legs twisted. His head nods to the side, cushions prop him up but his eyes don't leak so much and we understand each other perfectly well.

THE LEICESTER WRITES SHORT STORY PRIZE 2020

Swimming Against the Tide
CLAIRE SHERET

People used to say she swam like a fish. Her father said it was primal.

'After all, you grew inside that sac of fluid in your mother's belly for nine months before bein' pulled out glistenin' an' a-strugglin' for air. Jus' like the catch o' the day!'

Annie smiled at the memory of his words. She certainly was happiest when she was in the water. In her youth she'd swum competitively and had won medals for it. But right now, the living room walls were closing in on her. Squeezing tightly.

Annie stared at the bedside clock willing the numbers to say 14:00. John would arrive to take her swimming then. They went every Friday but today was special. It was her birthday. She had been looking forward to the trip all morning and had already put her swimsuit on under her dress. She grabbed a rolled-up towel from her linen cupboard. She was impatient to get going.

'Come on John, where are you? These damn walls are driving me crazy!' she said, as she crossed the landing. Her voice punctured the silence. Like a stone dropped in water it changed the space around her, disturbing the stillness. She headed downstairs, wincing a little with each step. Her feet hurt today. Arthritis, she supposed. She had seen what age had done to friends. Their bent bodies confined to home. Hours turned into days which became weeks and then months. The only meaningful markers of time for them were the changing of the seasons.

Annie was determined that wouldn't happen to her. She wanted to keep active for as long as she could. But her body didn't move so easily now and even when it did, it wasn't always in the way she expected or wanted. She dreaded the onset of winter. It grew so cold and snow piled right up to her porch making it difficult to get out. She shook her head to try and dislodge the gloom that lurked at the edge of many days for her now. Like sea mist rolling in, it came from nowhere and enveloped her.

A pick-up door slammed, jolting her out of her thoughts. She peered through the living room blinds. It was John. 'At last!' she muttered as he strode up the steps to her door. She smiled at the sight of him, before going to let him in. They hugged. He smelled warm and familiar. A mix of aftershave, those menthol cigarettes she wished he wouldn't smoke so many of, and, just a hint of sweat.

'Hey Annie, Happy Birthday!' he said. 'All set? Then let's get going! I came the coastal route here. The surf's up a bit but it looks like we'll have a great afternoon for a swim.'

As he helped her into his truck, she pushed an unruly clump of hair out of his eyes. He was a good man. Kind and thoughtful. She was thankful he was here to help her. She often wondered what made a young man like him want to help old biddies like her. She'd never asked him. Maybe she would today.

Music was blaring from the truck's radio. John moved to turn it off, but she stopped him.

'Leave it. It makes me feel alive!' she laughed.

'You never cease to surprise me Annie. I never figured you for a rock fan!' John looked at her smiling before turning the volume up, checking for her reaction. She smiled back so he left it and started singing along. Annie frowned and pretended to shield her ears, but the truth was the music added to her excitement at the trip. It reminded her of when she was a child. Her father used to take her, and her brother, to check his boat before they all headed for a swim. They would all sing along at the tops of their voices to the crooners on the radio. Annie breathed in deeply and could smell the salty, fishy warmth of her father's truck and hear his gravelly tones singing along to the swing band sounds.

John stopped singing and started talking to Annie about his morning. Annie stared out of the window not wanting to be distracted by his chatter. The noise of the truck and the music smothered some of his words and Annie's brain couldn't quite make sense of them. *Some benefits to getting old,* she thought, before telling herself off for being so selfish. She didn't mean to be. She was interested in what he had to say but she also wanted to savour every second of the journey to the bay. She was determined to enjoy this day. It might be one of the last swims they had before Fall.

John sensed Annie was lost in her own thoughts: 'That's enough of my stuff. I can see you want to enjoy the view, so I'll shut up now,' he said returning his attention to the music, humming and tapping the steering wheel in time to it.

Annie was uplifted by the brightness of the sky against the painted wooden homes which lined the main road out of town. The buildings reminded her of jellybeans and wildflowers. Even in the grey of winter the sight of them cheered her, making her feel less overwhelmed by the gloom. Like a cat in the sun, her body began to uncurl and relax.

She was as familiar with every crinkle of the coastline as she was with the lines on her face. But what always impressed her was the landscape's ability to adapt and change with the seasons. The grasses on the dunes had basked all summer long in the sun and would be bleached golden by now. But in a month or so they would die back, and the darkening sky would merge with the sea, giving the place a very different feel. Then a few months on from that tender new shoots would appear making everything look fresh and new again. Annie sighed.

'You okay there, Annie? You cold? Shall I put the windows up?' John asked, reaching for the button on the dashboard.

'No, no I'm fine. I was just thinking it's beautiful today but, in a month or so it will be so cold here, it fills your veins and makes you feel brittle enough to snap! Hard to believe that beauty just pushes right back up again in the spring. Nature sure trumps us on that score,' she said.

They rounded the bend on Seabright Road and the old lighthouse loomed into view. It reminded Annie of a church spire, but its familiar whitewashed walls and red tile roof were beacons for a very different congregation. Decommissioned since boats had sophisticated navigation equipment onboard, its beam lit the way for tourists these days. Stranger than that to Annie was the number who flocked to photograph the Riley house to the left of the lighthouse. Derelict it had finally surrendered to the weather and lay slumped against the grassy bank, like a weary old man taking a rest.

'Buildings are like people I guess?' Annie mused, suddenly feeling sad again.

'Beg pardon Annie. What's that you say?' said John.

'Look at that old house. The state it's in,' she said. 'You'd never guess it used to be brimming with life. As a child I often took shelter in that house. The Rileys, all ten of them, always made me and my brother welcome until the worst of the winter storms passed and we could finish our walk home from school. Now look at it. Broken and abandoned. Such a shame.'

'Nothing lasts forever I suppose,' said John. 'What happened to the Riley's?'

'Kids all grew up, moved away and when Ma and Pa Riley passed on none of them wanted to come back here. So, the place just fell into disrepair over the years. Makes me sad.'

'Well I guess it's cheaper to let that happen than do it up and make it habitable again,' said John. 'It's happened in other places along this coastline now there's no fishing industry here. Many families have moved to the city and beyond.'

'That's what I find so sad. What made you stay John?'

'I guess I'm like you Annie. I love this place too much. I'd be like a fish out of water in the city. Besides I wouldn't get to take lovely ladies like you swimming, would I?'

Annie laughed and as they turned off the main coastal road and onto Cove Lane her mood lifted and a fluttering in her stomach began to grow with intensity the nearer the bay they got. The pick-up rumbled over the dirt track, sending dust and stones flying. Annie turned her face to the open window. She could smell the fresh pine scent from the trees which clung to either side of the track. She let the cool breeze rush over her cheeks. It reminded her of the brush of her mother's eyelashes against her face when she was young – butterfly kisses her mother used to call them. Annie took another deep breath allowing the woody, salty air to fill her lungs. She imagined it seeping from there into her veins, pulsing through her body, like a shot of adrenaline.

The forest gave way to grey rocks worn smooth by the sea. Little piles of driftwood tossed aside by the tide cluttered the shoreline – nature's litter, Annie called it. She watched the gulls circling above as the bay came fully into view.

'I could float right out of this truck window to join them if it wasn't for this damn seatbelt anchoring me down!' she said.

John laughed and as they pulled into the parking lot, Annie snapped open her seatbelt. John instinctively threw his arm out across her as the pick-up lurched to a halt in the sand.

'You gotta stop doing that Annie! What are you like? One of these days you're gonna hit your head on the dashboard, then I'll be in real trouble!' He rolled his eyes as if to chide her, but she saw there was a smile in them too.

'Ah don't be fussing, I'm fine!' she said as he jumped out of the truck and came to help her down from the cab. 'Why thank you, kind sir,' she said smiling at him, taking his hand and feigning a curtsey as she slid off the seat onto the ground. The warm breeze knocked into her like a breaker against the seawall, making her gasp. The salt in the air pricked her face and her dress flapped against her like a sail in the wind. John steadied her so she could climb out of her dress. He folded it and placed it on the front seat of the truck.

'Shall we?' he said, offering her his arm again. Linking arms, they walked down to the water's edge. Once there she kicked off her sandals, enjoying the feel of the cool sand beneath her toes. John bent down, picked her sandals up and tossed them back up the beach so they wouldn't be carried away by the tide.

THE LEICESTER WRITES SHORT STORY PRIZE 2020

The water licked and curled around Annie's toes like icy kisses, tickling and making her squeal. She shuddered with the shock as the surf rushed up over her ankles and was soon frothing up to her knees. It reminded her of when she was a kid and she and her brother would race to be the first in the water. He never beat her, something she was always proud of. The memory emboldened her, and she took a few steps further in to the water, until it came to the middle of her thighs. When she tried to look down at her feet, she became a little unsteady, so she concentrated on the horizon, watching the incoming waves rise and fall before they expired along the shoreline.

'You sure you want to swim today, it's choppier than it was earlier?' said John. The wind stole her reply, so she shouted it again and gave him a thumbs up gesture to be sure he understood. Further along the beach two young women were dithering, venturing into the sea then retreating. 'Wimps!' she growled under her breath as she picked her way with care, going deeper into the ocean until she felt her body move with the swell of the tide. John offered her his arm again, but this time she declined, surrendering herself to the waves, laughing as they engulfed her.

The cold of the water was like a slap. She tensed her body in shock then forced it to relax. Slowly she began to swim, raising one arm up and over, followed by the other one, kicking her feet until she fell into rhythm with the waves. Moving with increasing ease, she sliced through the water spurred on by the rhythmic one, two, count she had learned as a child, quickly putting more distance between herself and John. She thought she heard him call out, telling her to take it easy. But her body was working now and lost in a familiar pattern. Muscles and joints moving in unison. Just as they should. The gentle buffeting of the waves reminded her of being rocked. Not like a baby in a cradle. More like being in the arms of a new lover. Supported but never quite sure what might happen next. Alive and alert.

She stopped and began to tread water to take in the view. The rocky outcrops of land made her think of an octopus, its tentacles stretched out lying in wait for prey. She changed to breaststroke so she could keep moving but continue to look at the shoreline. Sometimes the land was a slumbering monster to her, waiting for her to stumble and fall. But out here in the silky infinite smoothness she was free and unfettered. Out here she was like any other swimmer. A small dot bobbing on the wide horizon. And with each stroke she pushed away the years.

Above, the gulls chattered. Their noise like echoes from the past. Her brother's shouts as they raced each other into the water. Her parents' voices urging them to take care. Cheering poolside crowds from her youth as she powered to victory. Giggling children running free, enjoying summer picnics and Thanksgiving fireworks on the beach. Triumphant trawlers sounding their return home full of fish. The boisterous banter of happy men spending hard-earned cash in the quayside bar before heading home to share the bounty with grateful and relieved families. Sounds of life being lived.

Annie's attention came back to the present as she scanned the shore again, noticing the two women she had seen earlier had dressed and moved along the beach. They were talking animatedly to John. Even from this distance she could tell they were young, in their early twenties. Their skinny jeans hugged their lean and supple limbs. Their beach blonde hair fanned out in the breeze like the streamers on top of the surf shack at the end of the beach.

'Look at them. Like moths to a flame!' she said aloud.

She wished they'd go away. They reminded her of how much she had lost. *I used to be you,* she thought. Suddenly she was aware her arms were becoming heavy. She struggled to make progress and realised she had swum out much further than usual. The tide had caught her. She saw John had stopped talking to the women and was swimming out to meet her.

'You okay?' he called. 'I thought I saw you waving your arms?'

'What are you talking about? I'm fine!' she rasped as he reached her. 'I'm not a child! Now out of my way. I want to go back to the shore.'

She knew she had overstretched herself this time. She was tired and cold. She needed to get out of the water. Thankfully she soon reached the shallows. Exhausted, she let the waves carry her in for the last few metres. She steadied herself with her hands on the shifting shingle, trying to avoid grazing her knees. She saw the two women were still there and wished again that they'd go away.

'Wait there, I'll help you,' John said.

His words had the impact of a life vest being punctured. The water tossed and rolled her like driftwood on the beach. The shingle scraped her making her knees bleed. She grimaced as the saltwater stung her broken skin. Struggling to turn and sit up she felt as floundering and helpless as a newborn at the feet of the two young women.

'Quit gawping!' she spat, not wanting to make eye contact with them for fear of the pity she was certain she would see on their faces.

John helped her up.

'Sorry Ma'am.' said the taller one. 'We just wanted to say we only hope we're as ballsy as you when we're your age.'

'John told us it was your eightieth birthday,' added the other.

Annie paused. It wasn't what she had expected them to say.

'Well you only get one life girls,' she blurted out, embarrassed.

John had fetched her towel and clothes and Annie let the two young women help her dress. Then John walked her back to the truck supporting her as she clambered up into the cab.

'You okay Annie?' he said. 'Did the girls upset you? You seemed flustered back there.'

'I'm fine John. They got me thinking, is all. You know, I'm the same person I was when I was their age.' *Just this damn body that's changed,* she muttered to herself.

John climbed in the truck and was about to start the engine, when Annie stopped him. 'Can we just look awhile?' she said, blinking as if to burn imprints of the bay in her mind, like photographs to be flicked through later.

THE LEICESTER WRITES SHORT STORY PRIZE 2020

The Reddifers
PETER HANKINS

The iPad was gone in a moment. Dad had been holding it high, trying to get the perfect angle for a selfie (he did those, when the occasion called for it). The two of us stood on the old iron bridge with the broad canal and Chesney's factory behind us; the highlight of the old, circular walk we used to do every Sunday morning ('faithfully but not religiously' as Dad used to say) while Mum was cooking the roast. Then the motorbike hammered past us – wham! – it must have been doing at least eighty - right on the edge of the road. Dad was concentrating on framing his shot and didn't see the bike till it slammed past where we stood on the narrow pavement, near enough to make his old brown jacket flap in the wind of its passage; he recoiled convulsively and somehow the iPad slipped from his grasp, landed once with a sharp crack on the iron parapet of the bridge, and fell into the black water below.

Dad stared – we both stared - then he put his hands on the parapet (studded with bolts, painted pale blue) and tried to lift one leg to climb up; for a man of his age that wasn't easy, and he hadn't got anywhere before I pulled him back.

'Dad! Don't be stupid! It's gone!' I said. He looked at me in distress and then he lowered his eyes and drooped as if some vital energy had fallen from him as well as his tablet.

THE LEICESTER WRITES SHORT STORY PRIZE 2020

I took it for granted then that in trying to climb onto the parapet he was just trying to get a better look at where the iPad had fallen, that some idea of going down to the canal side and retrieving it had gripped his mind in the first shock of his loss. I knew the device had become important to him, but I did not imagine yet that, following a moment's reflection, he might have decided that once it had gone the best course, taken all round, was to throw himself after it.

When Mum died, I had feared that Dad wouldn't cope. He had come to depend on her. She had always been in charge at home – done all the work, she would have said, not inaccurately, though it was pretty clear to me that while she resented the responsibility of organising every detail of their shared life, she also relished the dominance it gave her. Outside their little semi-detached council house it might have been different once. Before he retired, Dad went out to the warehouse every day, and there, in that world, he had been a significant figure, the person who made things happen. No-one knew the procedures like he did; no-one else could remember catalogue numbers without looking them up. At home, though, it was absolutely Mum who was the boss, and it always had been. Mum maintained contact with friends and family, organised the annual holiday, choosing both timing and destination; she kept the chequebook and doled out Dad's pocket money; she picked out, bought, washed and laid out Dad's clothes for him; she fed him as and how she thought best and told him where he was to go and when. Once he retired, he sank entirely into the domestic regime and stopped making any decisions, ever; he lay back under Mum's management as if he had become a baby, though I never saw him throw a tantrum. He seemed to like it that way, or perhaps he simply couldn't imagine it being otherwise. Once, in a restaurant, I saw Mum grow impatient with his hesitation; she snatched the menu from his hand and ordered for him. I thought that was going a bit far; how they got on between themselves at home was one thing: to humiliate him in front of a waiter like that seemed cruel. But he waved at me dismissively when I started to protest and assured me with a smile that it was fine.

'She knows what I want,' he said.

'I know a sight better than you do anyway, you soft 'aporth,' said Mum smiling, and they both laughed, in perfect accord.

So when Mum abruptly decided it was time to die, and acted on that conclusion without mucking about (one decisive stroke; she never woke up), I feared that Dad wouldn't know how to live any more. There was no way that I, or anyone else, could step into her shoes for him. I was afraid he might feel obliged to follow her lead and quietly pass away, if he could work out how to do it without her supervision.

But instead, in his own way, step by step, he adjusted. He did not begin to make decisions for himself; instead, he arranged his life so as to make them unnecessary. He fell into a rigid weekly and daily cycle, getting up at 6.05 and breakfasting on Weetabix, then there'd be a mug of Nescafé Gold Blend instant coffee with a single digestive at 11.00, a sandwich of Kingsmill soft medium-sliced white bread and Cathedral City mature cheddar at 12.30, PG Tips and a single bourbon biscuit at 15.00 hours, and dinner at 6.30 (menu according to a fixed weekly cycle). Each day would close with a mug of Milo and bed at 9.30. He wore the same clothes in a rotating weekly cycle, and went up town once a month where he would get anything he needed, not that there was ever much. He went to coffee morning on Tuesday and the working men's club on Thursday - because it was quieter than on Friday, and he liked it quiet. He never went on holiday. Bank Holidays, birthdays, and any other occasional festivities, were times of trouble and embarrassment to him, and he tried to minimise or ignore them as far as he could. He was always happy to receive visits, and you would always get a cup of tea, but you could not get a meal from him unless it was Friday, when you could have fish and chips. They would of course be eaten with tea, the beverage of choice to accompany all meals.

He simplified the business of conversation, too. He generally told the same anecdotes according to the occasion, with very small variations. There were six core tales that came round again and again, and about ten more that only got the occasional outing. If not relating one of his set pieces he would generally listen patiently, with no great pretence of being interested, to anything you might choose to say. There were fixed forms of words which he would use for various social milestones; his arrival ('good morrow, Squire'), for drinking tea ('the cup that cheers'), for announcing his departure ('Well, I reckon I ought to sling me hook'), for actually departing, usually about twenty minutes later ('I'll say cheerio, then'), and so on. These had to be observed. When I opened my front door to him, he would say:

'Can I come in? It's only me.'

I would say:

'Is it you, then?'

He would reply:

'It was when I came out.'

Once, I happened to be standing outside the front door talking to Mrs Margate next door when he arrived. He stood at the gate, foxed by this, but Mrs Margate was in full flood; she wasn't going to be finished for a couple of minutes at least. I waved him in, and he reluctantly edged past me and into the house. Mrs Margate politely conceded at last that she had better let me go and popped back inside. There we were, Dad and me - except the wrong way round, him inside, me outside.

'Can I come in?' he said, uncomfortably, 'It's only me.'

'I know it's you, Dad,' I said, 'I can see it's you, can't I? And you don't need to come in. You're already in, aren't you?'

He just looked at me unhappily and waited in silence. I suddenly felt rather cruel.

'Well, fair enough I suppose. Is it you then?' I said.

THE LEICESTER WRITES SHORT STORY PRIZE 2020

'It was when I came out,' he said, with a look of the purest relief on his face, and turned to go into the living room.

I wasn't sure Dad would take to the iPad, but I thought he really needed access to the online world or he would get left behind when they closed the Post Office, and not be able to deal with his bills or his pension. A tablet seemed a likelier bet than trying to get him to engage with a desk top computer – a kind of device which he scorned and secretly feared – or a smart phone. Talking about phones invariably triggered anecdote number 5, anyway, and I could do without hearing that one again.

As it turned out, he took to the tablet fairly well, developing a strong but limited attachment to the thing. No matter what I said, he would not use it to order his groceries online (perhaps because he thought he would have had to switch to Tesco, though I don't think he would have used the Co-op online either) or to do any other kind of shopping. He took to email quite readily, but either could not or would not engage with social media of any kind. He did not want to listen to music or watch videos, nor even to catch up on TV programmes. That last one was a bit disappointing. Since Mum died, he had taken to watching a great deal of television, including a lot of serials and quizzes, programmes that Mum had always dismissed as tripe. That had surprised me a bit, because I had always taken Dad to be the more intellectual of the two, on the quiet. He was a great reader when he was younger, and if he had been born into a later generation I felt sure he would have gone to university instead of leaving school after his GCSEs. He used to talk to me about books when I was a kid, and he had strong and original opinions, often with a bit of a political slant – he was scathing about fairytale royalty that never did a hand's turn, and rude about princesses in a way that made me laugh. I particularly remember what he said about *Treasure Island*. According to Dad, Long John Silver was a good man, trapped by a poisonous socioeconomic system. Dad had a whole imagined backstory in which the young Silver and his wife built up a farm in the West Indies which was then expropriated by the local landlord. In Dad's version, Long John swore an oath to follow the pirates until he had four thousand silver Spanish dollars in compensation, hence the name he went by. Dr Livesey, on the other hand, was 'a complete Tory bastard' according to Dad, and I still believe that Robert Louis Stevenson, in his own mind, thought the same. At any rate, Dad would not consider using his iPad to keep up with soap operas.

What he really took to was his 'reddifers'.

Dad saw the point of a calendar app right away, using it to schedule his iron-clad routine and give him reminders of what to do next. That was all very well, but at first he found that these reminders would take him by surprise, telling him to go to the coffee morning, say, when he was there already. He found this deeply confusing. For Dad the breakthrough was realising that he could simply schedule a separate event earlier on, which told him it was time to get 'ready for' coffee morning, or a shopping trip. These were his 'reddifers'. This way, you could have a string or network of reminders for the same event; one might tell you to get your bag ready, the other that it was time to set out. Moreover, and this was where the whole thing really took off, you could have reddifers for reddifers, second-order reddifers, as it were, ones that told you to set further reminders, or reminders for reminders. Given the regularity of his habits now, he could set reddifers to recur weekly or daily and map out his whole future life with ease.

This innovation enabled Dad to dispense with paper calendars and many scribbled notes. He carried the iPad around with him constantly, and at night he laid it carefully on the pillow where Mum's head had once rested. Gradually more and more of his routine fell under the management of the reddifers. I did not realise how far this process had gone until about a year after he had started with it all, when he proudly showed me part of the system. By then it was so elaborate I found it quite hard to follow.

'Why is watching *Strictly Come Dancing* shown as a reddifer?' I asked, 'Isn't that just a thing you want to do?'

'That tripe?' said Dad, 'No, I shouldn't watch that for myself. But I need to, so I'm ready for talking to Mrs Mount about it.'

It turned out that nearly all of Dad's TV viewing was just a mass of reddifers, preparation for his appearances at coffee morning or the club.

What I hadn't fully realised was how in building up the reddifers, Dad had not copied his memory so much as transferred it. The growing reddifer system had slowly eroded his recollection and initiative. It was, in fact, a stick he could no longer walk without.

Then, of course, thanks to some bastard on a motorbike, it went into the canal. When we got back home afterwards, Dad sat down, pale and miserable, and gave up comprehensively all at once, on everything. We sat for some time, without my being able to trigger any of the usual anecdotes, or anything much in the way of unscripted conversation.

'Time for your tea, then, Dad?' I said at last.

'I don't know what I'm to eat,' he said.

'It's Saturday! You know what you have on a Saturday!'

But he wouldn't be drawn. I made him his baked beans on toast, which he ate while I watched; then I left him, but I was worried and came back the next morning. I found him still sitting in his chair; he hadn't been to bed, or washed, or changed his clothes, or eaten.

And so it went for the next few days. If he was supervised, he would go through his old routine in a hangdog sort of way, barely speaking; once left, he sat down and did nothing. I had to take time off work to see to him; at first I thought he would get over it, but there were no signs of him recovering his initiative. On Tuesday, I took him to the usual coffee morning, but when I came back to get him, Mrs

Mount drew me aside and asked discreetly whether he was ill or upset.

'We haven't been able to get a word out of him,' she said, 'I always ask him about *Strictly*, because I know he likes it. Daft programme if you ask me, all bare-chested young men with long, greasy hair. Anton's all right. Hope your dad's not sickening?'

I bought Dad a new iPad, with some reluctance as it seemed like procuring more drugs for someone who'd just had a bad experience with them; but it didn't do any good. For a while we managed with me looking in on him mornings and evenings, and him sitting still all day, but it couldn't last. In the end, he had to go into a home where he could be properly supervised, and there he still is.

Or is he? Is he really there? Is it Dad, or just his vacant body that sits in the home – the nonplussed human animal that played host to his mind for so many years? Was it actually not just a tablet but in fact in every sense that really matters, *my Dad* who fell into the canal after cracking his screen on the bridge? It is certainly true that if I could somehow recover that iPad from the water and miraculously get it to work again, I could give it to an actor who would be able to perform a flawless imitation of Dad's later life, going where Dad would have gone, saying what Dad would have said, and so on. But no; it wouldn't really be him. I don't believe he is to be found in either the old folks' home or the canal. I think the truth is that he went some time ago and in that last stage of his life, Dad was merely performing a stereotyped imitation of himself. At some earlier point the real Dad, his soul or his inward personhood, escaped somehow, leaving his automaton body and his programmed routines as a decoy. He ghosted us, silently disappearing from our lives; perhaps he even ghosted himself and doesn't yet know that he's gone, will never know.

This is a strange and unsettling business, and for a while I should say I grieved as though he were dead. But I do not now believe I need to be too unhappy about the way things are. What I have finally come to think about it is this, more or less: that somewhere, somehow, Dad got the silver dollars that discharged his life's secret obligations - whatever *they* were; I wish I knew - and was free to go. He quietly slipped away - who can say where? But I believe it was a fulfilment, not a termination.

Still, I wish he'd been able to let me know when he thought he ought to sling his hook for the last time; I wish there had been a way to mark the final 'cheerio, then' - the one he really meant.

THE LEICESTER WRITES SHORT STORY PRIZE 2020

Required Reading
LAURA BLAKE

The table was set, laden with hot buttered crumpets and Mrs. Ada May's best china teacups laid out on freshly washed doilies. Each club member liked her tea just so, and Ada went through the list in her head; three and a half sugars for Victoria, with lashings of milk; black, with a wedge of lemon, for Elizabeth; and one sugar for Jane, because decorum prevented her from asking for a second. Anne's opinion on tea, which for her was a new and exciting novelty, was as radical as her opinions on political reform, and Boudicca only drank mead.

Jane Austen could always be counted on to arrive early; she accepted her tea with a polite sigh ('one sugar, just how you like it,' Ada said with an arch smile) and began to stack a small pile of books on the table. Jane could also be counted on to devour the supplementary reading list in its entirety. Elizabeth Taylor floated in on a silken cloud, dispensing air kisses and leaving a trail of elegant French smoke in her wake. Queen Victoria liked to be announced, but this was trumped by Boudicca's arrival, who rode right up to the table on a horse.

'Sorry I'm late,' said Anne Boleyn, haughtily dropping into an empty chair. 'Lizzie said she was going to come this time, but she's off kinging again.'

Jane rolled her eyes. Elizabeth the First had made an awful lot of fuss about wanting to join the book club, even asking that they re-arrange their monthly meetings around her schedule, but so far yet she had to attend a single session. Anne caught the eye roll, and cattily remarked that she was afraid Jane was looking a touch *bilious*, and was she feeling well enough to chair the meeting?

Jane and Anne did not get on; Jane pitied Anne's choices, while Anne believed that the novelist thought far too highly of herself. Victoria often reminded them that they both died tragically; one at the hands of her husband, the other without any husband at all, so there was no need for the air of superiority on either of their parts, especially while *she* was in their presence. Victoria wasn't a founding member of the book club; she had merely wandered into the meeting one day and demanded she be given a teacup and allowed to stay. She rarely did the required reading, and was content to sit, sip tea and work on her sampler, and completely dominate the conversation whenever she liked, as she believed was her right.

Jane was about to respond with a cutting remark, but she was beaten by Ada; a shrewd woman who had raised seven children and diffused countless, trivial arguments in her time.

'Tea, Anne?' she asked, and Anne immediately brightened.

'Please. I'll try… green again. But six sugars this time; five wasn't quite palatable.' The perfect hostess, Ada didn't baulk, but nodded and passed the sugar bowl down the table.

'Now that we're all here...' Jane began, calling the meeting to order. There was a quiet rummaging as books were retrieved from handbags, cigarettes were lit and half-eaten crumpets pushed aside. Jane rapped her knuckles on a well-worn copy of *The Handmaid's Tale*.

'So, what did we think?'

The book club had, quite naturally, been of Jane's invention, but it had been Boudicca who'd inspired it. The warrior woman had been keen to learn how humanity – particularly its women – had fared in her absence, and had raided the library on a mission to discover what she'd missed since her untimely death.

Ada, who just so happened to work in the library, had been happy to amass a large selection of history books for Boudicca that covered everything from the Fall of the Roman Empire to the Clinton Scandal. Ada had left the woman, tall and proud, her face streaked with woad, at a small table with the books and whispered that she would be at the front desk if Boudicca needed anything further, then went back to work stamping and sorting and nudging her co-worker, Jane (who was curled up next to the storage heater with a Mills & Boon) every five minutes with her toe.

Presently Boudicca returned to the desk, looking put out.

'I'm sorry to disturb you,' she boomed, 'but these books bore me. So many tomes dedicated to petty men and their silly arguments. They can't get anything done. The Battle of the Monongahela River, for example, 'she thumbed noisily through a book and pointed at the offending page, 'any woman with an ounce of sense would have seen that this plan was doomed from the start.'

'Well,' Ada answered, 'that may be so, but there weren't any women at that battle. Or any of them, really. It wasn't the thing.'

'No women in battle? What nonsense is this?'

If Boudicca had had her way, she wouldn't have died when she did; ideally, she would have been victorious in her quest to finally rid her lands of the cowering, snivelling, invading Roman scum who'd had the gall to underestimate the Queen of the Iceni tribe, the bastards – but she had assumed that other women would have risen in her place to take up the fight.

The truth, as discovered that afternoon in the library, was eye-opening.

'House… wife?' She'd asked of Ada, dumbfounded.

'That's right,' Ada beamed, neat as a pin in her floral blouse and cameo brooch.

'You defended the home from raiders while your husband-slash-king was off in battle?'

'Not exactly… though my George did do his bit during the Second World War. Mind, none of the women on our road would have stood for a German Invasion. Irene Bruce at number forty-four had just bought a wireless – she *never* would have surrendered her house to the Jerries.'

'This displeases me,' said Boudicca, leaning heavily on the desk. 'Tell me everything.'

And Ada had done the best she could, explaining the notion of the patriarchy, the persecution of witches and the Suffragettes' long and (at this point Boudicca cheered slightly) occasionally violent fight for the vote, but her own knowledge was lacking – 'in my day, all you needed was your three R's and the ability to sew a straight seam,' she had apologised – and Boudicca quickly grew frustrated.

'Burnt, beaten, denied a vote,' she complained, 'how you have suffered, and for so long! At what point did you lose your way?'

'I don't know,' Ada floundered.

'You let the men have all the fun –'

'I know it looks a bit grim, from where you're sitting,' Ada said, 'but we women fought plenty of battles too, you know–'

'Did you bathe in the blood of your enemies?' Boudicca asked delightedly.

'Not exactly – what I mean is that there are plenty of women who stood up for equal rights, and that sort of thing, and while they didn't always succeed in their time, they certainly paved the way for others–'

'Then you shall teach me, Mrs. May,' Boudicca said cheerfully, crashing a large hand onto Ada's shoulder. 'You shall tell me the stories of my daughters' daughters, and I shall rejoice in their attempts, victories or no, to rid themselves of tyranny and oppression.'

'Well I would,' said Ada, 'but I'm not sure I'm the best person for the job–'

'I am though,' said Jane from beneath the desk. Jane had been listening intently to the conversation and had waited politely for an opportune moment to interject. She stood up and bobbed a curtsey.

'My name is Jane, and I know the kind of stories you'll want to listen to.

That's how it began, though at first the meetings consisted of Jane leading Boudicca and Ada on a whistle-stop tour of noted women throughout history, with the latter doing their best to keep up. Boudicca hadn't at all liked how each woman was discussed in relation to her marital status – 'we are here to learn about the women, not the men they submitted to' – but Jane had insisted it was important for context.

'You have to remember,' Jane said, from the comfort of her favourite chaise lounge, 'that for the longest time a woman's only role was to marry. And yet here we have Elizabeth Tudor, who ruled an entire country without a husband, and Margaret Thatcher, who managed a whole Government *and* a family at the same time. Women have been subverting the rules imposed on them by the patriarchy for centuries, and that's bloody brilliant, if you ask me.'

'Like you,' Boudicca said suddenly. 'You're not nearly as demure as you make out to be. You're quite forthright. No,

I mean that as a compliment.' And Jane did her best not to blush.

'I was required to publish my novels anonymously for fear they'd think me unladylike,' she admitted with a smile. 'But it turns out you can *really* let rip when you're unidentifiable.'

'I loved your stories, when I was a girl,' Ada said dreamily. '*And* the television adaptations. Colin in that wet shirt…'

'What did you write about?' Boudicca asked, as Ada sighed wistfully to herself.

'I pushed my George in the duck pond once, but it didn't quite have the same effect…'

'Love; marriage; the ridiculous constraints placed on single women, that sort of thing,' Jane replied.

'Then,' Boudicca decided, 'I should very much like to read your work.'

And that is how the history lesson became a book club, although Jane – who, despite being outspoken, was still a woman shaped by polite Regency society – insisted they start with the work of one of her contemporaries, rather than her own.

A week later, Ada was working her usual Tuesday afternoon shift in the library. She adored her job; it was the first one she'd had since she'd worked in the greengrocers at the age of seventeen. There, she'd weighed out potatoes and polished the scales, kept grubby little hands away from the apples and served a handsome chap named George who came in every Saturday morning for cigarettes and innocent flirtation. For ten consecutive weeks, he enquired after her health as he pushed three bob towards her, and she'd responded with 'fine, thank you,' as she slid a carton of Woodbines over to him. On the eleventh Saturday he surprised her by pushing a shiny gold band across the worn counter and she'd dropped his carton of cigarettes in shock. The greengrocer despaired – Ada was the fifth shop girl he'd lost in a year – but she'd been blissfully happy. The first three children came in quick succession, followed by the war, in which George dutifully played his part, and Ada dutifully did her best to 'make do' and 'carry on', and then George came home with a medal and Ada was so pleased to have him back that another three children were born by the decade's end (the fourth was conceived during George's all too brief leave in a questionable hotel in Brighton). Then the children grew up, and moved away, and produced children and grandchildren of their own, and Ada had yearned to feel useful again. The library gave her a specific sense of purpose she'd not known since she'd swapped the weighing scales for a lifetime of domestic placidity.

Ada hummed to herself as she sorted a stack of newly returned books. A polite cough caught her attention and she glanced upwards, her mouth falling open. Standing at the desk was the most beautiful woman she'd ever encountered.

'Excuse me,' said the woman in a soft, relaxed drawl, 'I'm looking for *Wuthering Heights,* but it doesn't appear to be on the shelf.'

'You won't find it, I'm afraid,' Ada responded, feeling guilty for inconveniencing the beautiful stranger, and wondering if that was something the woman experienced a lot. Did people go out of their way for her, just because she had a classically pleasing face?

'All three copies have been taken out for our first book club meeting.'

'When will it be available?' asked the woman. 'I'm auditioning, you see, for the role of Cathy. And so far the song, while rather catchy, hasn't been very useful in getting to the heart of Cathy's *motive*. Why does she want to go through the window so badly? What's wrong with the front door?'

Ada didn't know how to respond (she was only up to chapter two) but she promised to set a copy of the book aside as soon as the first meeting was over.

'In fact,' Ada said, hitting on an idea – she *really* didn't want to send the woman away completely empty handed – 'why don't you join us? We'll be exploring a different text each month to learn about noted female authors and the impact they had on society – perhaps you'll find it interesting?'

That was how Elizabeth Taylor joined the book club, and they'd acquired Anne not long after.

'*Jayne Eyre*?' Anne had said, holding up her own copy and raising one eyebrow after Jane had asked if she was in the wrong room. 'Where the wife gets displaced by the help? It's kind of my thing.'

They met in the back room of the library, every third Thursday. Although Jane chaired the meeting, it was Ada who served as unofficial hostess, a role she created for herself after listening to Jane critique *Wuthering Heights* for three hours with no thought for a tea break. The club members were nothing alike, but that's what, in Ada's opinion at least, made the meetings so *fun*. Anne was particularly well versed in witch lore, and had led an interesting session in all the ways Rowling got it right, while Elizabeth had moved them all to tears with a heart-wrenching rendition of Emily Barret Browning's *The Cry of the Children*. Jane had divulged how her unfinished novel ended and, on more than one occasion, Victoria had read aloud from her diaries, shushing them whenever she came to a particularly juicy bit.

'So, what did we think?' Jane asked, and Boudicca jabbed her copy angrily.

'I found this book a fitting study on the weakness of the modern woman,' she began. 'They just... let it happen. In my day we would not have stood for such nonsense! I, Queen of the Iceni, would have rather died than see myself enslaved–'

'You did die,' Anne said witheringly, 'having failed to protect your people.'

'I avenged the rape of my daughters and killed men with my bare hands,' Boudicca bellowed, slamming her large fists into the table, 'they cowered before my breast!'

'They're not *that* big,' Anne muttered into her teacup.

'I think you make an excellent point,' said Jane diplomatically, but once incensed (the mead didn't help) there was no stopping Boudicca.

'Breeding machines. That's all society thinks you're good for, and this Margaret of Atwood agrees!'

'She doesn't agree, you nitwit, it's a social commentary on the subjugation of–'

'I rather consider it a warning. You know, there are still entire societies out there who believe women are the inferior sex–'

'Women are more than the roles assigned to them,' Ada said calmly. 'Isn't that what we've learned? Even when forced into the robe, Offred retains her sense of self. It's inspiring – her fight is our fight.'

'Fight?' Boudicca scorned. 'None of you fought the way *I* fought. I fought for freedom. But I didn't take on the swords of Rome so that you,' she gestured furiously to Elizabeth, 'could play dress up and *you*,' her arm swept across the table to Ada, 'could stay at home and *clean*. You're all so *weak*.'

'Some of us didn't need a sword to bring down our enemies,' Jane sniffed. 'Some of us had just as much success merely wielding a pen.'

Boudicca snorted. 'Oh, how I cower before your mighty quill.'

'You have no idea the power one has when one is considered the most beautiful woman on earth,' Elizabeth murmured.

'And what did you *do* with that power, hmm?'

'Why...' Elizabeth exhaled lazily, a cloud of blue smoke billowing from her lips, 'I let them look at me. It made them feel... special.'

'And Anne convinced a king to make up an entirely new religion for her!' Jane interjected.

'And lost her head in the process.'

'Must you bring that up *again*?' Anne admonished, shaking out her velvet sleeves. 'You seem to be forgetting that I *also* birthed England's mightiest queen–'

'Excuse me,' came an affronted sniff from the other end of the table. 'If anyone can claim the title of mightiest queen it is surely I. You're looking at the United Kingdom's longest serving monarch–'

Ada sipped her tea as the argument raged around her. She thought it wise not to mention Elizabeth the Second.

'Maybe it's *your* fault,' Anne said, glaring at Boudicca.

'My fault?'

'You were too strong. You bruised too many egos. Then you popped your clogs and the men thought 'quick, better subjugate them before *that* happens again'. Perhaps *you're* the one that set us back in the first place.'

'All we know,' Elizabeth said, before Boudicca had a chance to remove the knife from her belt, 'Is that at some point man convinced himself that women were inferior, and they have spent centuries trying to convince us of the same. Some of us even fell for it,' she finished sadly.

Ada patted Elizabeth's hand comfortingly. 'We've all struggled,' she said, 'Some, more than others. And some in terrible ways. But we've all helped, too. We laid the groundwork for the *next* generation of women. And is that not worth it?'

'It would be fascinating to explore this from a different perspective,' Jane began eagerly, but she was interrupted by a new voice from the doorway.

'Excuse me… is this the book club?'

'Come in, Mrs. Seacole!' Ada sang warmly, jumping to her feet. 'Ladies, this is Mary. Mary, how do you take your tea?'

THE LEICESTER WRITES SHORT STORY PRIZE 2020

Packing like a Brownie Guide
JUDITH WILSON

Kneeling, I tug at the zip and my fingers grasp softness.

I breathe bluebells, fresh-snipped, and I inhale a little harder.

No, the smell is sickly-sweet.

But I open up anyway - chest tightening, heart thumping - and I shout out loud.

Suspicions confirmed.

Clarissa swishes in and sweetly rubs my calves.

It must have happened last night, commuter flight, Schipol return to Heathrow. I was dog-tired. I'd grabbed my black suitcase, it's always red-ribbon-tied. An old trick, I know. Except great minds think alike because – this bag?

It's also red-ribbon-tied.

Tentatively, my fingers explore crinkled textures: acrylic knits and nylon blouses. Not the Italian separates *I* wear for business trips, plus patent leather shoes. I drag out a garment or two and hold them up, so tight the light shines through.

If I've mistakenly taken someone else's suitcase, then –

Is a stranger fiddling, right now, with mine?

I open my fingers and the clothing flops to the carpet, like fluid punctuation.

I poke again into the suitcase.

Who did this packing? Trainers jammed anyhow without a plastic bag in sight. The blouses are scrunched, and the undies mismatched. It's a tsunami of fabric, out of control. The disarray? It's churned my stomach.

I absent myself from the room.

Downstairs, I lie on the sofa and tussle the Saturday papers. I try to focus on the fashion pages, yet the newsprint twirls illegible before my eyes.

That suitcase? It's a zipped itch - waiting to be scratched.

I return pronto to the bedroom and in a flash, I spew its contents onto the bed. One seersucker skirt, two cheesecloth tops, three airport romances. Nothing specific to identify its owner – only the plain black suitcase, scarlet-ribbon-tied.

Just like mine.

I do the right thing. I phone Heathrow's handling agent and explain the mix-up. No one has reported missing baggage like this. The woman on the line, silver-voiced, requests returning it 'at my convenience.' But I've noon-to-midnight meetings and I don't have the time.

Come Friday, I'm flying Heathrow to Berlin.

I'll take it back then.

Meanwhile, I repack the bag; it's the least I can do. I pour a large vodka and I settle to my task. *Shoes first.* I pop to fetch organizers; then I arrange the squeaky slip-ons, heels to toe, just so. I roll socks and tuck them amongst the stretchy-waisted jeans. Soon everything is divinely wrapped in tissue paper, just like those shops on Bond Street. The case zips shut with an elegant sigh.

I down my final inch of vodka. *That was fun.*

Outside the window, it's a perfect autumn afternoon. The bronze-tipped leaves on the oak tree sway back-and-forth.

Later, I indulge in a spot of online retail therapy.

My red pencil skirt and silk T-shirt – now lost to someone else?

They're On Sale!

Every cloud has a silver lining, right?

I'm as good as my word and I return the suitcase to Heathrow. The woman on the desk, pen poised, wants my details. I say I'm running late.

(I've plenty of time. I'll be back tonight.)

But later, when my flight touches down and I tip-tap through baggage reclaim, hand luggage only, I eye the Information Board. I stand shoulder-to-shoulder with my fellow passengers and I watch the bags waltz joyfully on the carousel.

Grab a small black wheelie - quick as you like.

I glide through 'Nothing to Declare'. Soon, I'm speeding westwards into London, watching the glitter of Heathrow recede in the car's rearview mirror.

'Someone waiting for you at home?'

The Uber driver, he's caught my eye.

I pause before I answer. I'm picturing a masculine contour on my sofa, feet on the coffee table. No, forget that;

a beer bottle in hand, a chilled rose waiting for Yours Truly. Or, no, halt that. He's in bed: sleepy, TV flickering, waiting for sex.

'Sure,' I say.

I stare so hard the driver drops his gaze.

I let myself in. Clarissa softly rubs my calves.

'Hey, kitty.'

Best welcome home I've had in days.

Tonight – this one, certain-sure, belongs to a man.

I delve right in and my hands are shaking. This time, I lift out a charcoal wool suit, Marks & Spencer. A three-pack of new shirts, only the blue one worn. He should have picked the lilac! A navy V-neck, intimately scented with woody cologne.

I press my face to it and I breathe in deeply.

Next, I undo his purple wash bag with confident fingers. *It's not prying!*

A plastic toothbrush, condoms (unopened, oh dear) and a minty mouth-spray.

No other clues.

I restore everything to its rightful place, taking my time. The order I add to the interior gives me such peace. The only problem?

I can't return it to the handling agent. That woman might recognize me.

Twice in seven days might look careless.

This weekend, I visit Mum's flat. I've recently sold it; she died six months back. Until now, I haven't mustered the courage to sort her possessions but today, I'm on fire. This whole suitcase thing has filled me with joy.

We can all progress when the time comes, right?

At the council tip, I chuck ten bin bags; I've no room for Mum's bits and bobs.

Last from my car boot, foremost in my mind, is the man's suitcase.

Stripped of its contents, it arcs gracefully through the air.

I couldn't take it back, OK? So, I donated the guy's clothes to Oxfam. The sign proclaimed: 'Wanted: Quality Men's Attire'.

Thank heaven for small mercies!

I'm super-busy in the upcoming month. Sometimes I'm doing three European trips a week. Now I'm in the swing of things, it's child's play to scour the carousel flight after flight. Late evening is best. People are weary. Not concentrating.

I always pick black.

Sometimes it gets awkward. Once, I grabbed a suitcase and a woman's hand covered mine. Her grip was insistent, her palm moist.

'It's not your case.' Her stare was fiery, so I gave in.

Another time, a guy claimed the luggage.

'It's mine.' I pointed to an invisible mark. 'Hands off.'

I needed my fix. For a moment, our eyes danced. He was sexy. And I could see him thinking: 'Christ, have I had too much gin on board?' He acquiesced. I quivered for ages after that encounter. The thrill lasted all the way home.

I unpacked that bag on the kitchen table – I simply couldn't wait.

This time there was an unexpected surprise. Tucked between the pinstripes and the leather brogues, I found apricot silk knickers. No wonder he gave in! I pictured us unzipping together at the airport, his anxious breath on my neck, lacy bras amongst the City ties.

'*Of course* - your wife's,' I'd say if pressed. No kidding.

The truth is, I don't care *what* these people keep in their bags.

It's the thrill of the unknown that's intoxicating. I'm learning about the human race. What they pack, what they like. How they do it.

What they hide.

As each week has passed, I've begun to vary how I dispose of people's possessions. I've sold off several lots on Ebay. (That was fun.) If I discover a piece I covet, I'll wear it and love it. *Finders Keepers*. One day, Pam in the office enquired after a vintage Hermes scarf that I'd knotted nonchalantly, Parisian-style, around my neck.

'Where did you get it?' Fixing my eye. 'That design is so rare.'

I didn't know she was an aficionado! I didn't wear it again.

Most especially, I'm looking for personal items, those quirky pieces that tell the story of 'them'.

Once I even found a handwritten diary. (*That* guy had eclectic tastes.)

But most of all, I love the re-packing. I've spent a small fortune on new shirt envelopes, drawstring underwear tidies, a cache of 'laundry' bags.

Matching each appropriate container to each owner's clothing – it brings me such joy.

Let's face it: I'm doing them all a favour.

Some nights, I dream of returning the lost goods. I line up the owners, and they kneel. Opening the lost suitcase, they're so grateful. I point to exquisite layers of precision; socks tucked neatly, silk dresses rolled, ties curled like babies' toes.

I treat the ladies to gold tissue and black crinkles for the guys.

I show them how to pack, how to pack like a …

I was eight when I joined the Brownie Guides. The shared camaraderie enfolded me but most especially, I adored the uniform. Money was tight back home, but I didn't mind that Mum bought all my kit second hand. Yes, the fabric was washed paler than the traditional chestnut brown, and yes, it bore marks from the previous girl's badges. But I was quite used to the threads of someone else's nametapes scratching my neck.

Being a Brownie Guide meant *belonging*.

I immersed myself wholeheartedly. I completed all the badges and I rose to the rank of Sixer. I was a Leprechaun, which was fitting, given that Dad hailed from Ireland.

Then he ran off with his secretary and left Mum and me all alone.

After that, the Brownies came to an end. I guess Brown Owl felt sorry for me, because the day I left, she gifted me a Brownie Guide annual.

I read it from cover to cover.

My favourite section: 'How to Pack Like a Brownie Guide.'

Honestly? I've never looked back. In the dark days when Mum lost her job and after we were kicked out from our flat, I treasured the order that came with my ability to pack. As we moved from one temporary place to the next, knowing my suitcase was immaculate truly soothed me.

It was my version of clean knickers in case I got knocked down.

I studied hard; my CV is a thing of beauty. I earn a decent income and therefore I like to splurge on clothes, and I travel in style. I have the perfect capsule wardrobe. Of course, a man in my life would be the cherry on the cake.

But we can't have it all, right?

One thing, though. I really ought to stop taking people's things.

Tonight, I'm especially buoyant. I've had a tip-top meeting in Antwerp, and the flight is early for a change. I haven't whipped a bag in weeks. I've spotted a Samsonite. It's in my favourite colour, Schiaparelli pink, and I –

Well, I just fancy having a go.

Haven't I *earned* it?

I wait only a few minutes. It's fresh on the carousel.

No one challenges me as I lift the glowing rectangle and sail through Customs. I've been a little more daring than usual. But that's my game.

I'm the only player and I always win.

I'm almost out the other side when I feel a hand upon my shoulder.

The Customs Officer and I stare together at the sizzling pink suitcase.

'Over here please, Madam.'

Behind me, my fellow passengers stream past in fiery confluence.

'I think I've picked up the wrong one,' I say.

Why, oh why, didn't I stick with black?

'Can you open it please, Madam?'

I hope it's locked; that will help my lie. But it unzips seamlessly.

Together we stare at the interior, with its tight-pulled straps and an oyster silky lining. The arrangement of the clothes is so symmetrical. It's hard to tell, amongst the lambswool sweaters and blue denim, if these contents belong to a man or a woman.

It's Brownie Guide perfect.

I shiver a little. I only need to offload this suitcase and then –

'Wait here, Madam. We need to take a closer look.'

When the Customs Officer returns with a colleague, there are sniffer dogs.

I'm accompanied to an unmarked room.

'Did you pack this bag yourself, Madam?'

I'm sweating profusely. The clothes are so beautifully aligned. I can't -

'No, I didn't pack it. It's not mine - *honestly*.'

His eyes are cool. The spaniels are circling.

I hear another male voice from behind, clear and loud.

'It's cocaine, sir.'

'You're sure about that?'

I hold my breath and the room begins to spin.

'I'm sure, sir. A ton of coke - all of it, brilliantly packed.'

Faith
FIONA ENNIS

Some black stuff from the barbequed sausage sticks to my fingers, and I lick it off before it goes on my First Holy Communion dress. The sausage tastes really salty, and Mammy said I can only have one, that the man who owns the pub probably soaked them in salt-water the night before to make everyone drink more. That must be why the mammies and daddies are having all that wine and beer, or maybe it's because we're all melting from the sun here in the beer garden. I don't know why they call it a garden when it's made of concrete. In the corner, the bouncy castle is so full it wobbles, and when Sharon Power from my class climbs on, the little flags on its towers dip and go up again. The mammies fan themselves with Communion booklets and beer mats, and the daddies have pulled their white plasticky chairs away from the tables with the big umbrellas, and are facing the sun, their sleeves rolled up.

With my straw, I slurp the last drops of orange between the ice, then try to hand my glass to Mammy, but she's pulling at her blue dress and staring over at Brian again. He owns the bouncy castle, and she looked at him all day at the Easter party as well. Her make-up is melting in the heat, and looks all shiny, with black stuff smudged around her eyes, but if I tell her, she'll spend the next twenty minutes in the toilets fixing it up, and she already spent ages doing that.

She looks at me and takes my glass. 'Ava, have a go on the bouncy castle. It's only here for the day.'

'I want to see Daddy when he comes.'

'Well, his wife had better let him come this time. I'll keep an eye out. Go on.'

Brian stands near his bouncy castle, and I sit at the edge to take my shoes off, as far away from him as I can, but he lands beside me. He always helps the little girls take their shoes off, but I'm eight years old and can take off my own shoes. He takes my foot in his hand and undoes the buckle, and after he gently slips off that shoe, he takes my other leg and slides his hand all the way down to my frilly socks and slowly opens the clasp. I wriggle free as soon as he has the shoe off.

When I climb onto the bouncy castle, I get a spot near the front, to see Daddy as soon as he gets here. Our neighbour, Leah, is talking to Mammy and pointing at the black stuff around her eyes. Mammy waves to let me know she's going inside, must be to the toilets, even though she'd said she'd keep an eye out for Daddy. His sons or his wife must have made him bring them to the golf course or something, rather than spend time with me. They always do that, and it isn't fair. It just isn't.

Tears wet my cheeks and run down my neck to the collar of my dress. My breath catches every time I bounce, but when I stop to take a big breath in, Sharon Power's elbow whacks into my mouth, right into my gums, and it really hurts. I can taste blood. It's salty and warm and slides through the gap where my front baby teeth used to be, then drops onto my dress in red blobs. Sharon doesn't even say sorry, just glances around to check if anyone has seen and jumps up and down. When I slide off the castle, Brian stops me to say something, but I run to the bathroom to find Mammy.

She's leaning over the sink, face close to the mirror, putting pale stuff under her eyes.

'Mammy, look!' Blood splutters from my mouth.

'Ava! Are you okay? Spit in the sink and open your mouth for me... let me see... open wider... ah, okay... it's not too bad... you'll be fine in a few minutes.' Then she gives me a wad of toilet paper to hold to my mouth and dabs at the blood on the dress, but it won't come off, not even when she rubs it with wet toilet paper; tiny red bits just stick to the stain. She tucks more paper around the neck of my dress, walks into a cubicle and turns the lock.

Another door opens, and Niamh Hartley's mammy, Joan, goes to the sink and washes her hands. She's wearing a pink satin dress, but it's a bit small for her. I can see her belly through the material.

She says, 'Ah, Ava. What happened you?'

'Sharon Power banged into me.'

'You poor thing. Hang on a minute.' Joan roots in her bag and pulls a tenner out of her purse. 'This is for your Communion, but keep that tissue up to your mouth, there's a good girl, and I'll give the money to your mum when she's finished in there.'

'Thanks.'

She says, 'You must be rolling in it. What are you getting with all your Communion money?'

'A phone.'

'What would you want a phone for?'

'So I can talk to Daddy every night.'

'Oh. Is he here today?'

A toilet flushes, and Mammy walks out of the cubicle saying, 'He's coming later, if his wife lets him.'

Joan closes her bag. 'Well, in fairness, he was married with kids when you got mixed up with him.'

Mammy just looks in the mirror and washes her hands, while Joan walks out and forgets to leave the tenner. Hopefully she'll give it to me later.

Even though my mouth still hurts, it's nearly stopped bleeding. Mammy tries to rub the stain out of my dress again, but it won't budge. Then she pulls my Communion cardigan out of her bag. I don't want to wear it. It's boiling out, and anyway, the cardigan might look fluffy, but really, it's all itchy. My auntie knitted it, and Mammy said she only did it because all the family went to her son's Communion in Carlow, instead of mine. Even my granny went.

She hands it to me and says, 'Button it up to hide the stain.'

'But it's roasting out.'

'You can't go around looking like that.'

I close the shiny buttons and feel sweaty and scratchy. When we leave the bathroom, Mammy takes my hand, and that makes it okay.

She says, 'Mind your feet now, Ava. You shouldn't walk around without shoes. Lots of women here are wearing heels, and there's glass on the ground.'

'Okay, Mammy.'

'I don't know if the stain will come out of that dress.'

'I'm sorry.' I squeeze her hand, and she squeezes it back.

'Just be more careful.'

She waves at the mammies who are chatting, but walks past them to the bouncy castle, and stands near Brian.

He comes over and says, 'She okay? She got some clobber.'

Mammy says, 'She is, thanks.'

He says, 'You're looking well, Deirdre.'

'Feel like I'm about to melt.'

'Sure, we're not built for this weather. It's unnatural. Can I get you a drink?'

'Ah no, you're grand thanks.'

'Come on. What'll you have?'

'Well, a bottle of cider and a pint glass with ice would be lovely, thanks.'

He pats me on the head. 'I'll get this one an orange as well.'

I move from under his hand. When he's gone, Mammy takes out her phone and does her usual thing of pretending to take a photo, but really she's just looking at herself with the phone's camera.

I say, 'Mammy, will you text Daddy please?'

'He might not be coming.'

'But he said...'

'He's said lots of things.'

She ruffles her hair, then puts away her phone. When Brian comes back with the drinks, he hands me the orange with the straw, and Mammy takes a sip from her glass.

She says, 'You shouldn't have, Brian, but thanks.'

He says, 'No bother.'

'You're on the dry yourself?'

'Yeah, have to pack up the castle later and take it off in the van. Couldn't leave it overnight.'

'Ah, right.'

'Have to stay with it all day at these pub events. Last year, some eejit got mouldy, clambered onto it in her shoes and punctured it.'

'What a muppet. Some dose.'

'Can't complain though. I got an inflatable slide, and it's going down a treat for the Communions. I'm booked solid for the next few weekends.'

'How they can bounce up and down on rubber in this heat is beyond me. I'm hot just looking at them.'

'I bet you are.' He winks at Mammy, and they look at each other, but he nods at me. 'I'm doing a stint at *The Red Hen* next Saturday, and you're more than welcome to bring herself along. Same set-up as this.'

'Thanks, she'd love that.'

'What age is she anyway? She's pretty grown-up looking to be making her Communion.'

'Ah, she's like her mammy. Sure, I was in the clubs when I was only sixteen.'

'I'd believe it.' He smiles at Mammy, and she goes red, but he's watching me suck orange through my straw.

Mammy's phone rings, and she says, 'I'd better take this,' and walks off.

He turns to me and says, 'Are you not roasting in that cardigan? Would you not take it off so I can have a good look at you in that white dress?'

'Mammy says I have to wear it.'

He winks at me. 'Do you always do what you're told?'

'Yes.'

'Good girl.'

Mammy comes back and says, 'That was her dad, wondering where we are.'

I knew he'd come! I just knew it!

Brian says, 'Her dad?'

She says quickly, 'Oh, we're not together. He's bringing her off for the evening.'

Brian says, 'Oh, really?'

Mammy smiles and says, 'Yes, really,' and strokes his arm, but he's watching me again.

Then next thing, Daddy is here, and he looks lovely in his grey suit and pink shirt, and he's staring at Mammy, although not in the way he stares at her, like really stares, when she's not looking.

He says to Mammy and Brian, 'Not disturbing anything, am I?' He hugs me. 'Hi sweetheart.'

Brian says to Mammy, 'I'll keep an eye on this castle.' He clinks her glass.' See you in a bit.'

He walks away, and Daddy says to Mammy, 'Who's your man?'

She says, 'What's it to you?'

Then he turns and says to me, 'You look beautiful.'

She says, 'If you bring her for ice-cream, make sure she puts on a napkin.'

Daddy sees Mammy looking at Brian, then says, 'I'm afraid I won't be able to bring her off. Something's come up.'

He's only joking. He must be.

Mammy says, 'You can't do this. You didn't mention anything about it on the phone.'

'Can't be helped.' He hands me a card and smiles. 'There's a big voucher in there for Smyth's, and next weekend I'll pick you up and you can get whatever you like.'

I feel my face scrunch up.

Mammy says, 'Is this because of Brian?'

Daddy says, 'Oh, Brian, is it? No, it's nothing to do with him. I have to pick up the boys from the driving range.'

'Yeah, right.'

'Sorry if I've messed up your plans. But Ava wouldn't mind tagging along with you and what's-his-name, would you, sweetheart?'

I say, 'Daddy, please.'

He says, 'Look, I'm only upsetting her by staying.' Then he kisses me on the forehead and says, 'I'll make it up to you soon. Don't cry.'

Mammy leans towards him and whispers, but I can hear her. 'It's always the same with you, leaving me to do everything for her. When can I get a day off? Is that too much to ask for? Is it?'

He just walks away. Mammy's face is red, even under her makeup, and a tear slides down her cheek.

I take her hand, squeeze it, and say, 'I'm sorry, Mammy. I'm sorry,' but she won't squeeze it back.

THE LEICESTER WRITES SHORT STORY PRIZE 2020

Sarika and Me
RADHIKA PRAVEEN

Don't get me wrong. I never considered Sarika to be my friend. Perhaps, for her, I might have been one. More than a friend, actually. Today, she is leaving the country because her husband is dead.

Sarika was my neighbour. In fact, we shared a wall between our flats. I had moved to a two-bedroom, semi-furnished rental property in Harrow with my husband from a beautiful house in Aylesbury, which we'd let out to tenants. As first-time tenants *and* houseowners simultaneously, I can now say that I'd hated the experience. But then, thirteen years ago, I didn't have the luxury to love or hate. I was a part-time research student at a university in the city. I also had a temporary job. So this move was to facilitate my needs – to travel to work and study, without having to spend a lot of money or time in commuting.

The flat was, as we would call it in Mumbai, a *match-box*. Functional, with low ceilings characteristic of the new-build London flats, and no room for storage or imagination. It was comfortable, however, and accommodated essentials such as a bed and writing table, an electric cooker in the kitchen and a refrigerator, a few unsightly racks and a spiral staircase that led down to the allocated garbage and bin-bag areas. Here was the only space where the residents of this building made any social connections with each other, if at all, during the weekly garbage collection day.

A second gate from the refuse-area also led to the main road. And this was the bit of Harrow that I loved: it was lined by a row of bustling Asian grocery shops and so-called *Indian* restaurants that were in reality run by Bangladeshi, Nepalese, and Sri Lankan immigrants. The mini markets were chaotic, with too many uniformed staff members who spoke little or no English. Their goods were more far more overpriced than the Tesco Express or Sainsbury's Local down the road, but they were popular because they sold every Indian and Southeast Asian ingredient. During festive occasions, you could even find exotic items that would be impossible to obtain in your own native country. All you had to do was to look in the right places. Moreover, Indian food franchisees like Saravana Bhavan and Chennai Dosa operated proudly alongside Subway and KFC, while other restaurants here banked on their regular clientele who did not mind the flashy lights, dingy interiors and loud Bollywood music. It made me wonder how many of the workers here even had legal passports.

My part of Harrow was brown to the core. And each day, as I travelled on the white tube to a white London, I looked forward to coming back to this familiar shade of brownness. Besides, although most of the small business owners here had arrived a generation or two ago, like me, they wore a disoriented, unsettled look. Be they the elderly Gujarati immigrants from Uganda selling home-cooked methi theplas and roti-curry and syrupy jilebis; the Sri Lankan refugee greengrocers; Bihari or Bengali women working at beauty parlours; Pathans from Afghanistan and Pakistan selling Shawarma kebabs, or Sardarjis selling electric and plastic goods, chargers, and sim cards. Slowly but surely, Harrow was growing on me.

My first meeting with Sarika is unforgettable because it was completely comical. I saw her on my way home from the Metropolitan tube station, having finished a particularly draining day at the office. She drudged a few paces ahead of me, both her hands full of the bulky, green, and blue shopping carry-bags that were bursting at their seams. Her backpack sagged with what I assumed was a laptop, or heavy books, perhaps. As if these weren't enough, sticking out of one of the carry-bags was the jhadoo - an Indian fibre-broomstick, with a matching dustpan. Her bright blue trainers, which I later learnt, belonged to her young sister-in-law, were Heelys, and probably oversized.

I didn't know then that she was my neighbour. But the scene reminded me of the Indian cartoonist, Mario Miranda's endearing caricatures of women of all shapes and sizes on the murals on Mumbai's pubs and railway stations. I couldn't help but chuckle at the thought of home. Just then, her mobile rang. She appeared to panic as she struggled to get it out from her backpack. In the ensuing confusion, she missed an uneven slab and her shoes suddenly began to act like clumsy skates. Instinctively, I hurried forward and grabbed her just in time to steady herself, letting her possessions fall to the ground. She took a moment to gasp and heave, her free hand now at her chest, sputtering thankyous and sorrys all at once. I asked her if she was okay, picking up her vegetables and bags one by one, and suggested that she should probably answer her mobile, first, which was ringing now for the third time. She managed a weak smile at last, dug out an old blackberry from a zip in her backpack, and squinted her eyes at its screen to check who was calling. As she held the phone to her ear, I noticed her hands were still trembling. I decided to wait with her until her call was over.

She spoke Gujarati – a language I understood but wasn't fluent in. I'd gathered from her talks that there had been a misunderstanding with her husband. That he was supposed to pick her up from another shop elsewhere and she, upon not finding him where she was waiting, had decided to walk home by herself. *Typical*, I remember thinking to myself, *this is what most Indian husbands do.* Just two days ago, my own husband was so engrossed in conversation with a visiting, bachelor friend – about industrial effluents and chemicals polluting the rivers in the UK – that he forgot I was away at my evening class and didn't make dinner for the three of us!

'Thank you so much,' she said, at last, touching me at my elbow after disconnecting her call. She showed not the least bit of anger or frustration with her husband for having left her alone. 'I know you... you are my new neighbour from next door. We live in 4B. You are from India I know. From where? May I ask? Myself, Sarika, from Ahmedavad. Tame Gujarati cho?'

It was nearly a month since our move, so I admit, I was a little surprised by her candid introduction. I felt obliged to reply that I wasn't a Gujarati, and belonged to the south of India; although, I said I could understand a bit of her language as I'd spent my growing-up years in the multicultural Mumbai. There was a brief pause. I told her that we shared a wall between our flats. Was it her daughter, a little girl whom we couldn't help overhear often?

'Ohh, did she disturb you? So sorry...she's five only, so makes lot of noise. I must scold her if...'

'No-no, absolutely not. It is nice to hear her sweet voice, and she speaks your language so beautifully too! We don't mind if her voice travels over,' I said.

I'd lied of course. Every evening, we heard shouting from next door: mostly between women. Sometimes, a male voice interrupted, silencing them for good.

We climbed the stairs of our building together and reached our house on the fourth floor. I waited until she rang her doorbell so I could rid myself of her bags. An elderly lady in a white saree opened the door and a child came running to greet her mother as well.

'This is my Ba – my mother-in-law, and my daughter, Kinjal,' she introduced. They seemed to be friendly and extended an invitation for tea on the weekend.

'That would be nice, thank you,' I smiled politely, joining my hands in a Namaste to greet the old woman. 'I better go now, I've to catch up with some homework,' I said.

'Homework? So you're student? That's why...you speak good English! What subject? Science?' Sarika asked. I explained that I was studying the life of women in ancient India, while working part-time. This, she interpreted to *Ba* who nodded without any interest.

'Where is my son, didn't he arrive with you?' she sternly asked Sarika in Gujarati instead, adding, 'You ought to have prepared dinner if you were going to chat with your new friends. Now look, he'll have nothing to eat when he's home. You know that he's severely diabetic...' I could tell that the conversation was probably going to get more tense, so I excused myself, leaving an awkward Sarika to defend herself all alone.

I met Sarika almost every evening as our travel times often coincided. While the bickering next door continued each night, we never brought it up during our walks from the tube station. I'd observed that she was adept at applying layers of foundation under her makeup; on some days these were patchy, and I would spot, with concern, the purplish blues and greens of a bruise. I was aware that she worked as a dinner lady at a primary school a few miles away, and suspected if she was bullied at her workplace as well. But, of course, I didn't want to interfere. On the contrary, after my accidental exposure to Ba's displeasure towards her a few weeks ago, Sarika had begun to treat me as a confidante rather than being embarrassed or evasive about her family. She seemed to take abuse in her stride as if it were the most normal thing to do. I wondered if she was really being brave, or foolishly ignorant.

I tried my best to tilt our conversations away from family matters, turning them to food and recipes, or my current topic of research. I was surprised that Sarika didn't know about Vishakanyas, and explained that they were poison-damsels who existed in India around 300 to 400 BCE, if not earlier.

'Han, the Hindi movie na, Vishkanya? I've heard it.'

'No, no,' I laughed. 'The Visha-kanyas. They were used as political assassins in Chandragupta Maurya's kingdom. Girls from this community were carefully exposed to small quantities of various poisons from an early age through spices like nutmeg, certain stones and herbs. Some young girls died early in the process, but those who survived developed a resistance for it, such that their bodily fluids turned toxic.'

'What does that mean? You couldn't touch them?'

'Well, you could touch them, but anybody they had intercourse with, died instantly.'

Sarika began to laugh aloud. 'All this... research... sounds nice... in stories. I've heard enough of them in Gujarat ... for me, there is one Vishakanya – in my own house!'

'I didn't get it...'

'Why do you need to research that far? Today also, as women, we are fed poison everyday…of fear, shame... Look at Ba, she tried to kill my daughter when she was born because she was a girl.'

'Oh, come on, Sarika. Are you serious?'

'Aur kya? My husband interfered...he told her, 'Ba, this is the first child. We will try again', and that is when she stopped...'

I gave up trying. She had drawn me into a negative discussion about her family again.

I tried to keep away, but Sarika began to share food with us – hot dhoklas or sweets that she'd prepared. She was undoubtedly a great cook, but an unappreciated one. Her husband, born and brought up in the UK, worked at the till in Sainsburys. Theirs' was an arranged marriage: Sarika's family had wanted a groom settled abroad, and her husband's family, first-time immigrants themselves, sought a bride from India who could cook well and wouldn't be the kind to 'break' a marriage. She told me this herself.

'It makes perfect sense,' I remarked, not without sarcasm. She justified it in her own way.

'They have seen so many marriages break up, ending in divorce. Their nephews, nieces...many are separated. Actually, I'm not surprised.' She began to whisper, 'their men cannot do anything on their own. Not even pick one glass of water by themselves! So spoilt, so spoilt.'

The dividing wall between both our flats could barely conceal the voices of either residents. I found it fascinating that Sarika was well aware of this. *How could a person be mature as well as indifferent to injustice?* I pictured the mother-in-law in the house next door, her ear pressed on the wall to catch what her daughter-in-law was saying about her.

'Sarika, how many years have you been married?'

'Twelve. In the beginning all was fine. But after Kinjal…' her breath trailed off, 'they almost killed her,' she choked.

This time I didn't know if I should believe her.

Sarika took a deep breath, smiling suddenly. 'Anyways, forget all that. Can you guess why I made this sweet today?'

'Why?' I asked.

'I'm pregnant! Fourth month already!' she squeezed my arm, excited.

'Do they know?'

'Yes, yes. My Ba is giving me good food to eat. Lots of badam, kesar and milk. She expects the baby boy to be fair, no less.'

'Ha! Don't have too many almonds, though, or nutmeg!' I laughed, and asked: 'How do you know…that it'll be a boy?'

'Shhh….she'll hear you! It *is* going to be a boy this time, I convinced her….chokas. I told her I had a dream about Devi Ma. That s*he* told me it'll be a boy.' She chuckled mischievously. 'Ba is very religious…'

Somehow, I had a bad feeling that evening. Sarika was bright and intelligent, but she wasn't capable of deceiving anybody. Less than a month later, I wasn't surprised to hear that Sarika had suffered a miscarriage. That is when I decided to take matters into my own hands.

I saw Sarika again after a few weeks, walking with her daughter. They were heading towards the main street, which was decorated with lights and displayed colourful clay diya-pots, six-pack sets of rangoli powders, ornaments for the goddess, as well as for little girls. Sarika, however, seemed oblivious to these. Dazed and withdrawn, she did not notice her daughter's absence even when Kinjal left her grip to run to me.

'Mummy, look, it's Aunty from 4A!'

I lifted Kinjal in my arms and walked to Sarika. She had lost a lot of weight.

'How have you been?' I asked.

'Can I speak to you?' she asked me straight away. 'Not your home, they can hear us,' she added, before I could answer.

'Hmm,' I nodded. 'In that case, we'll make sure that we're not heard,' I smiled, holding her by her shoulder and giving her a squeeze.

'Let's finish our Navaratri shopping first? We'll head home and let Kinjal play.' I chose a pair of shiny bangles and a box of red and black kunnikuru beads for her to make DIY necklaces with.

After we reached the building, I told Kinjal to bring her craft kit, as I had a surprise for her. By the time the little girl arrived with Sarika, I'd prepared some ginger-masala-chai and poured them into two cups. I'd also set the music volume to its highest, and played some old Bollywood songs. Kinjal enjoyed this, and danced and clapped her hands in tune to the music.

'My husband is seeing someone,' Sarika said quietly.

She was slouched on the chair. Bringing her hands together now, she broke down. I held her and took her to the kitchen so that Kinjal wouldn't get upset.

'Sarika, do you think your mother-in-law knows?' I asked her, half expecting the answer.

'Yes. She set it up herself. She will do anything for a grandson...' she paused, sobbing. 'I know she did it. *She caused my miscarriage...I just know it.*'

'You should go to the police, Sarika,' I firmly suggested, but she shook her head.

'Not easy. I cannot prove she did that, but I know she has. All those glasses of badam milk she forced me to have... But after the sonography report, I got smell of strong jaiphal in the milk. *Everyday*. I fell sick, I was saying nonsense... You'd warned, remember? You told me not to have nutmeg.'

I let Sarika cry until she was calm again. Having to handle someone like her, was exhausting. Thankfully, Kinjal ran into the kitchen. She was hungry. I gave her some biscuits, and handed her the box of beads and bangles as well, which I'd gift-wrapped.

'Why these? You shouldn't have bothered,' Sarika said softly, and turned to her daughter.

'Did you thank Aunty, beta?' The girl suddenly became very shy. I gave her a cuddle and helped her to open the packet.

'Kinjal, we used to play with these seeds when we were children. They lasted long, but we had to throw them immediately if they broke or cracked accidentally, or got damaged. Will you remember to do that?' I asked Kinjal. She nodded, and ran away, leaving the packet with Sarika.

'Yes, I know these…I've seen these plants in Gujarat. Ratti, they are called. Ba uses them for prayers too,' she said.

After they left, I shut the door, seriously evaluating Sarika's place in my life. I promised to plunge into my projects and assessments, now that we were approaching the year-end.

The next fortnight, however, Sarika's husband died of cardiac arrest. He'd passed away in his sleep. 'Just like his father…my only son,' Ba wailed aloud when my husband and I visited them to pay our respects.

Today, 13 days after the incident, Sarika knocked on my door again. She looked peaceful, and even had something positive to say about the cold weather. She held my hands in hers, and said that she was leaving for Gujarat with Kinjal, to her parents. 'Let the old woman rot alone. I just came to say… thank you, for everything.'

'Bye…' I said, but she was gone.

I opened my hands. She'd returned the packet of ratti seeds, although it looked like some were missing.

THE LEICESTER WRITES SHORT STORY PRIZE 2020

Steel Hearts
HARJIT KEANU SINGH

Do steel hearts bleed?

It was *the* modern question – akin to the classic conundrum of dreaming androids and electric sheep. And yet nobody was ever interested in the answers - just the search for them, the questions themselves and the other questions they usually bore. Do steel hearts bleed? Who was it meant for? Why did it matter? If they did, would that be so bad? Some people would like to see androids with a weakness to them. The question was just another version of a question, packaged and made more suitable for the times. What it really referred to was emotion, the dangers of it. Was it worse to feel too much or nothing at all? *That* was the true question. A lot of people asked and so one could assume a lot of people cared. Maybe that's why it mattered.

But for some it didn't matter all that greatly. For some maybe it all mattered too much. For Iris it didn't matter at all.

The young tanned man's eyes snapped open. There was no fluttering of the eyes, nor some yawn as he blinked into daylight. For him morning came as a sudden intrusion. Black became blue. Night had turned to dawn. Sleep just stopped. Silence was cut short by the song of civilisation - from the hum of hover-cars and chirping claims from billboard advertisements.

'Good morning Iris,' came a disembodied voice that ghosted over his apartment in its calm yet sterile tone. A blue light emanated from the lines between his walls and the corners of his apartment, flaring in brightness whenever his smarthome spoke. 'This is your daily alarm. The time is seven-thirty A.M and the temperature in Stardust City is sixty-three degrees Fahrenheit.' Iris had shut away his hazel eyes. *Out of sight, out of mind*, isn't that the old saying? *'Please wake up Iris.'* His blinds began to automatically open and so sunlight scrubbed the shadows of the ceiling away inch by inch.

'Snooze.'

'You have disallowed the snooze feature,' responded the voice of his smarthome. Iris sighed in response. His metallic arm reached out for his second pillow and pressed it against his face. He drowned himself in darkness, hoping to dive deep into some sweet slumber to escape from a day that had barely begun. *'Please wake up Iris.'*

Fucking no-snooze feature he thought. Even his thoughts came at him in that tired growl of a voice that only the early morning could bring.

'Please wake up Iris,' the voice repeated. It sounded sharper. Iris pressed himself deeper into the pillow, trying to spend another slice of morning to seep himself in something. He only now realised too late that he was not diving into a sea of slumber once again, but was now sinking in a vast ocean of bitter cold consciousness. His smarthome sounded louder. The sounds of the city came at him harsher. Soft

morning light fell on steel and skin. Forget starting to sink, now he had started to drown, only just grasping at the futility of fighting back against those waves of wakefulness.

Iris sighed again.

'Please wake up Iris.'
Jesus Christ.
'Please wake up Iris.'
No.
'Please wake up Iris.'
Fuck off.
'Please wake up Iris.'

'Okay!' snapped Iris, the pillow moved from over his face, steel fingers gripping the fabric so tight that he felt like he could tear it apart. Lines embedded in his arms like makeshift veins began to glow red as he flared with anger. His eyes scanned the ceiling, seeing the blue lights in the lines between his walls and ceiling begin to fade away. His arms lit up as amber. 'I'm sorry.' The voice didn't respond. Iris scanned the ceiling. He asked himself, *is it worse to feel too much or feel nothing at all?* He didn't know why, it just suddenly came to him. A part of him flushed. Was he really feeling sorry for his smarthome? He sighed.

'*Searching…*' responded the voice, the lights flaring up again, becoming bright and then fading, dancing to his ghostial voice.

'What are you searching for?' asked Iris, suddenly sitting up in interest.

'Common answers to your question, 'is it worse to feel too much or feel nothing at all?' said the voice.

'What?' Iris' dark brows furrowed in confusion as he looked up around his home. His arms returned back to that crimson glow. Some smarthomes were sophisticated but he was not rich enough to get one that read his thoughts. But he didn't say anything out loud. Did he? He resisted the urge to yawn, the familiar fatigue of the morning clouding his thoughts. 'Cancel the search.'

'Cancelled.'

Iris stood up and stretched, only feeling relief from his back, not his arms. Ten years and he never got used to that feeling, the relief from everywhere but his arms. A steel finger brushed his arm, tracing one of the lines from shoulder to his twist - metal on metal.

It was his morning ritual.

Some wanted a cup of coffee.

Others desired their implants.

Iris craved touch.

So he let his finger rub his arm, letting it do its dance on the steel. He read that some cultures had dances hundreds of years ago to summon rain. Maybe this was his own dance, a finger tracing an etched line from his shoulder to his wrist, a rain to summon...Happiness? Love? There were no words to describe defeating loneliness.

He just wanted to make sure he could still feel something, his presence, that special softness of someone against you, something. He could still feel everything, just not that small stretching relief. The lines in his steel arms glowed yellow as he submitted to his contemplations. Iris looked away, so focused on ignoring them that he didn't even get the brief reprieve when the lights died down.

'Shower on,' commanded Iris, as he walked into his ensuite bathroom, the one other room in his small apartment.

When the fuck did I leave this on?

A flare of anger rose in him and the several lines formed in his arms began to gleam red as he saw a simple seat hovering in the air before his desk. He tapped a button on the armrests and let it slowly float down and rest on a pad underneath it where lights danced on a surface and a word appeared on it:

HOVER SEAT NOW CHARGING: 3%.

Iris stepped into the bathroom as water spilled from the shower head into the small cubicle of a glassed off shower area his bathroom space would allow. He stopped looking so angry when he caught himself in the mirror, the glow of his arms dying down again as he stripped off his clothes. The brief shower did little to wake him up. 'Shower off. Catch me up on the news.'

'In recent news…' Iris ignored the voice as he clothed himself again, he only wanted a voice to fill the void and he was tired of his own already. He picked up a thick transparent bracelet, letting it lock around his right hand as he began to move his fingers, commanding his toothbrush

to float through the air. *'Initialism has risen three-percent since last year, the movement whereby people identify themselves by initials rather than full names has seen...'*

His smarthome continued as he began brushing his teeth. He stared at himself in the mirror. He usually slicked back his short dark hair, which was currently a mess this morning. His eyes scanned over his face, his short nose, the thin lips, reminding himself to shave as the spectre of a beard, in the form of stubble. He looked at himself, fingers twitching as he moved his toothbrush back and forth, neck moving as he breathed. He looked like a person, but so did androids and holograms nowadays.

Was he a person? He didn't feel like it sometimes. He felt like something that had garnered the worst parts of a person - the neediness, the sadness, the vitriol and desperation of it all. He swore that sometimes, the way crying could be unending, the way anger could be so uncontrollable, he could get drunk on feeling; not on lust nor desire, but feeling, the pure rawness of emotion itself.

And the suffering made him hate it, and the elation made him love it.

Iris blinked suddenly realising he was crying. That happened often, more often than he'd like. He shut his eyes and gave himself a moment, shrugging off the feeling as he opened his palm and let his toothbrush fly into his hand as he spat into the sink.

'...trend of Breakfast is returning with over sixty-percent of citizens saying they were open to having breakfast in the morning. The classic practice used to be…'

'Mirror on.' The mirror lit up, as a holographic screen appeared overlaying the glass presenting a set of numerous icons. Iris could still see his reflection underneath. He tapped one without even having to look as he focused on brushing his teeth, and the screen shifted instantly.

'...other news, a government bill sponsored by global digital security corporation Panoptes was passed last month and is soon to go into effect…' Iris only heard the voice briefly as he scrolled through the timeline, before finding something he could distract himself on. A square appeared, popping off the screen with a thin white holographic tendril that connected back to the screen. The square read:

Good morning Iris! You have two reminders!

Iris tapped the square and watched it disappear before the holographic screen displayed its first reminder in another popping square, hovering close to Iris' face.

Reminder (Today):
Anniversary. Get mom some flowers.

His mother was dead. She had been dead for ten years. She was gone and nothing was going to bring her back.

Except everything else did. The memory of her laughter. That emptiness from a lack of her embrace. The deep sound of her singing voice over some lullaby. The sunrises she had never seen, and the starry nights he knew she'd love.

Everything else always did. Sometimes Iris wished that he could forget all about her. He always felt bad for thinking about it afterwards. But he still did, only sometimes, on nights so cold that he'd be frozen forever like some macabre statue, the exhibit of the lonely and grief-stricken.

Iris' arms radiated red at the thought about that upcoming visit to the dead. He tried to concentrate on anything else, other than his reflection, other than seeing how sad he looked; how childlike. And thinking of himself as a child only made him think of his mom and that…

He gripped the sink tightly. The ceramic began to sound strained, the pressure from his steely fingertips causing a crack in the sink. There was a reason most of his things, his toothbrush and hairbrush couldn't be held, and instead floated in the air, responding to the most minute movements of his hand.

The reminder repeated in Iris' mind as he took a moment to collect himself. He swiped the text away allowing the next reminder to come up and replace it:

Reminder (Today):
Dad's going to die.

Iris slapped the words away. He stopped looking at the mirror. He almost forgot that *everything* was going to change today.

It suddenly felt like a chore to even stand. Tears welled up. Breathing became hard.

Maybe it was better to feel nothing at all.

THE LEICESTER WRITES SHORT STORY PRIZE 2020

Bottled Up
MATT KENDRICK

In those six months off work, I didn't brush my hair. I left it loose and it would whip about me in the blustery winds as I walked, each afternoon, along the beach. I liked the sea spray's bite against my cheeks. I liked the squelch of seaweed underfoot.

I scoured the sand for souvenirs. One time, I found a peacock feather and wondered how it got there. I collected seashells with a thought to doing something creative with them. My best find was a message in a bottle. Blue, frosted glass – I guess it was a gin bottle before it was requisitioned as a love note's reliquary.

I took it home and unscrewed the top. I prised out the message and held it in my hands. The paper was dry. It smelled of juniper berries and sea salt.

'My dearest Angela,' wrote the letter writer. 'You disappeared without saying goodbye. I tried calling but your phone went straight to voicemail. I must have left you thirty messages by now and I apologise for the angry ones. Sleep has been difficult. I've kept the indent in your pillow just as it was when I woke and realised you were gone. The wardrobe is full of your clothes. A strand of your silvery hair still clogs the shower drain.'

I stopped there and pictured them – Patrick, the letter writer, and Angela, the woman with the silvery hair. I imagined them awkwardly holding hands on their first date;

eating ice-cream at the seaside; a proposal, a wedding, a small disagreement escalating into door slamming, reconciling with hungry kisses. The message gave no reason why Angela might have left as she did.

After reading it twice, I furled the paper back into the bottle and set the bottle on the cabinet in the living room. It caught the sun and dappled the wall with turquoise patches. On a whim, I inserted the peacock feather and skirted the base with shells so it became an arrangement of seaside souvenirs.

They encroached on the framed photo of Danny, my secondary school boyfriend, and the empty goldfish bowl I bought the day I won the goldfish at the fair. The goldfish was called Danny after the secondary school boyfriend. He (secondary school Danny) cheated on me with a girl from chess club. Goldfish Danny did no such thing. He just got tired of living. I kept the bowl to remind me of him flitting in endless circles round his glassy prison. I kept the photo of secondary school Danny to remind me everything rusts in the end.

A few days before finding the bottle, I found a grey hair and twirled it through my fingers. When I go on holiday, I send myself postcards whose sun-drenched images pale after a couple of years stuck on the fridge. I have Grandmother's wedding ring in my jewellery box. The gold-plating is tarnished and infused with Mother's voice telling me it might someday be my something old.

I used to imagine it when I closed my eyes at night – the organ playing the wedding march, walking down the aisle towards Danny. But Danny kept on cheating. After the girl from chess club came a pale-skinned junkie whose eyes looked like death; then a tongue-studded emo; then an on-off affair with a travel agent from Greatham. He was faithful for a few months before he faltered once again. In the end, he was lured in by a hairdresser who tottered about on five inch heels. She got pregnant. She told me to fuck off when I confronted her outside her shop.

I bet Patrick never cheated. As I contemplated the bottle, I realised it was blue and borrowed and old and new altogether – so it was a much better omen for a happy marriage than Grandmother's tarnished ring. I realised, too, that I knew the names Patrick and Angela. Their story was in the papers in my final year at school. It was at a point after Danny had made out with the chess club hussy. Enrique Iglesias was all over the radio and the popular girls were wearing military crop tops and cargo trousers.

On a slow news day, the front page was dedicated to a woman who had disappeared in the night. 'Without a trace,' claimed the headline. A small scale police operation was instigated due to the suspicious nature of her disappearance. She didn't take any clothes with her. She didn't tell anyone where she was going. They took Patrick in for questioning if I remember it correctly. Then Angela was snapped by a speed camera heading south on the A15. Sometime after that, Patrick must have written his message in a bottle.

'I will wait for you,' he wrote. 'I will watch the lapping of the waves under autumn sunsets. I will remember how you dived in the sea on the day we drove out to Saltburn and had the whole beach to ourselves. I will walk along the sands and feel the touch of your fingers brushing against my own. I will hold your laughter in my heart. Perhaps one day, I will find your answer in another bottle, telling me you will return.'

Having figured out the letter writer's identity, I found a grainy image of the happy couple online. Angela's body was angled slightly away from Patrick and her expression was restless. Patrick, meanwhile, was wreathed in a ruddy glow. His pupils were dilated; his smile extended outwards from his mouth. I imagined him rushing through every room of the house on the morning after Angela disappeared; tapping his fingers on the interview desk at the police station; trembling as he looked out to sea, a single tear trickling down his cheek.

A Google search revealed he still worked in town as an architect. His headshot on the company website showed confidence and the picture drew me in. Those full lips, his hair stylishly ungroomed, his left eyebrow slightly raised. The corners of his mouth were turned down when I zoomed in. And that was what made me decide, the next day, to walk to his office rather than taking my usual route along the beach. The sun was peeking out from behind the clouds and I noticed the glint of a lost earring on the pavement. I picked it up and slipped it in my pocket. I once found a tiara on the beach.

Outside the office building, I thought about ringing the buzzer but it didn't seem like the right thing to do. Instead, I found a spot where I could perch on a railing and watch for Patrick to come out for his lunch break. It reminded me of staking out the youth club when I was younger; how I shivered in the cold for two hours waiting for Danny's chess club hussy. I saw her in town not long ago. She still had the marks where my fingernails dug into her skin.

I left my mark on all of them in a way. The junkie, the emo, the travel agent. I put it about that the junkie had the clap and I scratched a key across the travel agent's car. It was only the hairdresser that sent curses back in my direction. Spiteful curses. They were the reason I ended up at the doctor's surgery with a medication pot and a sick note; which led me to taking my walks along the beach; which led me to finding the message in the bottle; which led me to staking out Patrick's office building.

He emerged just before one o'clock in a duffel coat and a tartan scarf. He walked quickly and I followed at a distance. He stopped at a cash point and checked his reflection in a shop window. I wondered how much he relied on routine to get him through the day. I wondered whether knowing his bottled message hadn't reached its destination would break him. I hoped that it would not.

The restaurant where he stopped for lunch was that fancy bistro in the square. He took a table by the window and I watched him through the glass. He looked at his watch then his phone. He squinted through the window and for a moment his gaze rested on me. Too briefly. I wish I could have made a postcard of that moment to add to my collection on the fridge.

It was a surprise when the woman turned up. She had her back to me. Blonde hair hung down past her shoulders and I thought it might be Angela returned from wherever she disappeared to before Patrick sent his heartbreak out to sea. From a different perspective, though, I could see it was not. The angle of her nose was not right. Her face was too angular. Just like Angela, there was a falseness to her smile.

I couldn't hear their words but I could see the faltering pauses of their conversation. She giggled more than seemed natural. He bit his lip and paid unwarranted attention to the menu. He ordered fish and chips while she had a salad. She pinched chips from his plate and they eased into each other's company. My shoulders tensed at an accidental meeting of their fingers simultaneously reaching for the salt pot. My lips pursed as they shared a chocolate dessert. They kissed. And, after that, I turned and walked back home.

I took the message in a bottle from its place on the living room cabinet. I yanked out the peacock feather and let it drift to the ground. It only took me ten minutes to get to the beach and, once I was there, I found a rock where I could smash the bottle. Glass shards cascaded to the sand. I stamped on them. I picked up the letter and ripped it into a hundred helpless pieces, fluttering away on the wind. Some of the pieces landed in the sea.

'I will wait for you,' he wrote. 'Forever and always, I will wait for you.'

The next day, I only made it out of bed to go to the toilet and make myself cups of tea. The day after that, I persuaded myself to the kitchen to raid the biscuit cupboard then forced myself to get dressed. I found the medication pot the doctor had given me when he signed me off work and I took a couple of pills. They made me feel calmer. It was a few days before I was back on the beach.

The wind was blowing a gale when I got there and I soon became a medusa with hair plastered to my face. I thought about the strand of grey. I wondered if I should get it dyed and considered what I would look like as a silvery blonde.

That afternoon, my haul of souvenirs included a dog tag and a seagull's egg. A baby's plastic dummy was swallowed up by the tide. Then, almost as if I'd conjured it, another bottle. Cloudy green glass whose message smelled of vinegar.

'My dearest Patrick,' wrote the letter writer. 'Perhaps you will give me a chance to explain.'

I never read the rest. But the bottle looks majestic on the living room cabinet with the peacock feather sticking out the top and the dog tag wrapped around its neck. With the tiara and the earring and the seashells and the seagull's egg, it makes quite a scene. There's no longer any room for the photo of Danny. So he now lives in the spare bedroom, trapped behind the goldfish bowl. I took my residual anger for the way he cheated on me and bottled it on a faded postcard of Torremolinos.

In the murk of a midwinter sunset, I cast it out to sea.

THE LEICESTER WRITES SHORT STORY PRIZE 2020

The Naughty Step
MAUREEN CULLEN

Chloe thumps down on the bottom step, hugging Haley-Two. Squeezing in a deep breath she grabs a fistful of Haley's jaggy curls, holds her out by the arms and looks into her big dolly blue eyes. Haley's in a bad mood. She's been naughty again. Chloe lets out her breath in a big sigh. Haley-One would never have gotten into this bother. The nice policewoman said Haley-Two was the exact same as Haley-One; she'd bought her from Asda from the very same shelf as her first Haley and not to worry. Chloe pinches Dolly's arms hard with her fingernails. This Haley isn't the same, Chloe can tell. You can't just replace people like that. They may say they're the same, but they really are not.

Like Daddy. Chloe sniffs, sits Haley down beside her, and squeezes Dolly's head hard so she balances on the step with her legs stuck out in front, sitting proper. 'No, Haley, you can't go out and buy another daddy, dress him up the same and pretend he's your new daddy.' Chloe shakes her head.

She taps a finger on her cheek. Daddy Jimmy was the first one, with the long lashes and brown eyes like Chloe. And the gold ring that slid up and down his shaky finger that sometimes rolled off and Chloe had to get down on her belly and fish it out of wherever it landed.

Mummy said not to miss Daddy after he left. Granny had already stopped coming cause *she wasn't having a druggie for a son-in-law.* Chloe picks up Haley and hugs her. There were no bedtime stories after Daddy left, no ice creams with chocolate sprinkles from the van and no more rides on his shoulders. When Chloe asked Mummy when he was coming back, she said he'd be lucky to be out in ten years. Despite the hug, Chloe's eyes nip, and she blinks fast to stop the tears.

Daddy Rick came next, a big fat slob who *ate us out of house and home,* spending all the benefits. Chloe shakes her head so fast her bunches smack her cheeks. He drank a lot of beers and was always shouting, so Chloe hid under the bed and clapped her hands to her ears so she couldn't hear the names he called Mummy. But that didn't work; they got into her head: *whore, cow, bitch…* Aargh.

Chloe puts on a prim face, looks down her nose and presses her lips tight. She points at Haley with her big finger. 'Daddy Jimmy was a druggie, and Daddy Rick was a bad, bad, man. Watch out Haley. Daddy-Three's back in the kitchen.'

Chloe huffs. She's with Haley on the naughty step every day, sometimes three times. Least it's nice and soft under her bottom, no hard, woody bits or splinters like at Mummy's. She rubs the carpet with a thumb and stretches so she can lay her head back on a higher step to look up the stairwell. From here she can see under her bed and all the toys and books scattered on the floor. Her photo album lives under that bed. On the cover is a thick white rose Chloe likes to trace with her finger. She's allowed to look in her album any time, but she only does it when she's alone. That way she and Mummy can be together.

'So there, Haley, even you don't get to see the page where Mummy smiles out from the swing in the park.' Mummy laughs and holds the rails, pushing up into the sky with her long blonde hair flowing behind her, like a princess. Her throat is so very white and thin, like milk, no blotches and no choking. No blood spurting. Chloe shivers. Haley-One didn't croak like Mummy when she got all cut up, but she still had to go away. She was evidence, the nice lady policewoman said.

Chloe turns the pages of her album in her mind. Daddy Jimmy is next, sitting on the couch smoking his special ciggies. His eyes are half closed; he looks all dreamy. The last time Chloe saw him was at the funeral. He was standing with a big man in a uniform. She heard the jangle of cuffs before she saw them come up to her. Daddy bent down to kiss her, but the big man jerked Daddy away. Daddy Rick didn't come to the funeral or the party afterwards. Least not while Chloe was there with Nice Lady-Two… or was it Three? Chloe titters. So many nice ladies to remember. *Here's the nice lady to talk to you Chloe, here's the nice lady to take you to the funeral Chloe, here's another nice lady to take you to see the nice man at the courthouse.* Chloe blows out hard, seems to her there's just too many nice ladies in the world and they all have that same smarmy smile. Chloe stretches her mouth wide and scrunches her eyes. Her tongue fits in the wet space between her top teeth.

She picks Haley up and holds her out in front. 'Naughty Haley.' Chloe shakes her hard. 'Bad, bad, girl.' She sits Dolly across her knee, pulls down her knickers and smacks her bottom hard. 'Ouch, ouch, take that, take that' she says, just like Emergency Mummy when Chloe peed down the new dress. Nice Lady-One or was it Two? took her in the car to meet Emergency Mummy. A photo of the old witch is in her album. Chloe crayoned all over her hook nose and drew a big boil on her chin with red pen. Holding Haley up round her waist Chloe kisses her cheek. Just like Emergency Mummy did after the smacking. Just like Emergency Mummy did whenever the nice ladies came with their papers and briefcases to see Chloe. But they only spoke to the old witch, not with Chloe who sat quietly with Haley.

The next page has Mummy Angie. Chloe loved Mummy Angie. She wasn't supposed to call Angie 'Mummy', but the other kids called her Mummy, so Chloe did too, no matter what the nice lady said at the time. Chloe sits up straight and puts on a posh voice. 'No Chloe, Angie isn't your mummy, you must call her Angie. When your new mummy comes along then you can call her Mummy. You can't stay with Angie. She's not your forever mummy.'

Chloe nips Haley hard on the shoulder, fixes her between her legs and presses both thumbs in Haley's eyes. She scrunches up her own face tight and does her quiet, ever so quiet, scream. Only Chloe and Haley can hear it.

'Haley, it wasn't fair, it wasn't fair. How come the other kids got to stay with Angie? I was a good girl there, but still had to leave. The nice lady who took me away wasn't a nice lady; she was a bitch, a fucking bitch. I wanted to bite her big fat leg. I want Angie. Angie was cool with her sparkly leggings and bovver boots and all the shiny studs in her ears.' Chloe sniffs, trying to remember… yes, lemons, Angie smelled like lemons, sharp and clean. She never minded pee either.

Now Chloe's always on the naughty step. Forever Mummy isn't in the album. You only go in the album when you disappear, so Chloe can remember you. Chloe thumps the bottom step with her heels. She could make this mummy disappear if she wanted. All she had to do was be really bad and like magic Chloe would be out of here for good and another nice lady would stick a smiley photo of Forever Mummy in her white rose book. There were lots of pages left. She picks up Haley, pinches her ear. Haley squeals. Chloe smacks her across the face. 'Shud up, shud up, shud up.'

Chloe leans against the bannister. Maybe she could get Daddy-Three to fight with Forever Mummy again. He said Forever Mummy shouldn't let Chloe tear up his papers when his back was turned, or steal the chocolate out the fridge, or scowl at him all the time. Or use sweary words. Mummy told him off. Chloe copies Forever Mummy's bossy voice. 'There's none of us perfect, Robert. Don't leave your papers lying around. And try harder, she's only a little girl.'

Chloe chuckles. He's a lazy bastard. He still leaves his papers lying around. 'Well, Haley, he's a big fat fucking bastard. He is, he is. I hate him.' She titters.

Forever Mummy said she can come off the naughty step when she's learned her lesson. And Chloe can smell the scones baking in the oven. Her tummy rumbles, she licks her lips. Mummy's lovely raspberry jam will already be on the table, beside the blue shiny plates with fishes on.

'Now Haley look at me, look at me.' She holds Haley by the forearms and looks straight in her face. 'No bad words? Do you hear me? No bastards, no bloody hells, and no more peeing your pants. Big happy face or you won't get a scone. Alright?' She tucks Haley under her arm. Then remembers. Forever Mummy doesn't mind wet pants.

Slippers pad from the kitchen; two smiley eyes look around the bannister at Haley and Chloe.

'Have you learned your lesson, Chloe?'

'Yes, Mummy.' Chloe wriggles, opening her eyes wide.

'And has Haley?'

Chloe shakes her head. 'No, Mummy. Haley's been saying bad words again.'

Mummy comes around the banister and says, 'Budge up Pet.'

Chloe shifts into the wall.

Mummy sits down, facing ahead. Chloe peeks out of one eye.

'We must try harder to teach Haley not to swear.'

'Yes, Mummy.'

'Shall we?'

'Yes, Mummy.'

Mummy puts her hand out and Chloe passes Haley over.

Mummy places Haley on her knee and strokes her hair. Haley smiles.

Mummy whispers, 'Haley, saying bad words will get you in a whole heap of trouble.' Haley nods.

'So, do you want to be in trouble?'

Haley shakes her head.

'Well, let's do better from now on.'

Haley smiles and nods. Mummy passes her back to Chloe, springs up, wipes down her apron and pulls Chloe to her feet. Her hand is ever so warm and ever so strong.

'Come precious girl, let's go get a scone.'

THE LEICESTER WRITES SHORT STORY PRIZE 2020

Velocity
FARHANA KHALIQUE

When Miss said we could drop the orange peel in the water we were shocked. Thirteen years of Thou Shalt Not Litter so swiftly overturned by the word "biodegradable" was thrilling. Like realising we were hundreds of miles from home and could stay up as late as we wanted, or munch as many packets of Golden Wonder or Opal Fruits as we liked, 'cause no one checked the dorms after midnight. No junk food now, though; we were too busy measuring the speed of a stream, which meant clipboards and stopwatches and lots of fruit.

We were Geography Field Tripping somewhere in the Lake District, supposedly learning about nature, while singing Spice Girls songs and comparing muddy boots and friendship bracelets, and keeping an eye on the moody clouds. And watching Miss Rashid turn an orange into curls of sunshine. She gave the first handful of peel and a stopwatch to Faiza. Faiza looked like she'd rather just have the orange. But Miss told her to pick four other kids and they'd be Team One. Each team would be at different points along the stream and we'd compare notes at the end.

Faiza picked Jess, Nathalie, Beena and...

'Iram.'

Me? I looked up and forced myself to smile.

I had gone to the same primary school as Faiza and she was alright then. We'd sit together at dinnertime and I'd give her the fruit from my lunchbox and she'd give me the pakoras from hers. I couldn't believe she'd swap something homemade for just something that Dad would bring home from his shop. Sometimes I mixed things up a little by tempting her with a pomegranate or a kiwi fruit, but what Faiza liked best was oranges. Oh well, as long as I got something flaky and oniony and potatoey, I wasn't gonna question my luck. Mum didn't make samosas or pakoras any more, said she was too busy with work and it was easier just to buy them from Sainsbury's. She was always nice to Faiza's mum and would speak to her in Urdu and ask her if she missed Pakistan, and then they'd gossip for ages when they came to pick us up at the school gates. Later, when we were allowed to walk home by ourselves in Year Six, Faiza's place was on my way, so Mum told me to see that she got to her flat okay when we reached her estate before I came back to our house.

But at some point last year, after we started Lady Margaret's, Debbie had declared that Faiza had a big nose and laughed like a donkey. The first time she said it was in Form class and our Tutor was on the other side of the room, so only our side heard. Faiza stiffened and so did I. But everyone else laughed and Debbie sat back in her seat and twirled her hair, and then looked at me. So I swallowed the sourness in my mouth and joined in. Then it happened again a few weeks later in PE, when Jess missed a pass and spun goofily on one leg and everyone erupted, but one laugh ricocheted that little bit louder. Debbie grabbed the netball and paused. She muttered, 'Who let the donkey out', then smiled at the fresh wave of laughter and looked around the court. This time I didn't hesitate, and joined in. Joined in, and backed off. I mean, it was probably inevitable. Faiza was hopeless at PE, and not much better at anything else. And she still liked Boyzone, whereas the rest of us had moved onto Backstreet Boys and *NSYNC. And she really didn't help herself by fancying Mr Griffiths, who had a massive 'tache and never smiled. I mean, I know it's a girls' school, but you gotta have some standards. She made loud jokes in Science and nearly torched the lab once 'cause she was too busy looking at him and not at her Bunsen burner.

Now, next to a gushing stream in the middle of Cumbria, Faiza let me hold the stopwatch. 'Here you go,' she said.

I avoided her eyes. 'Thanks,' I said, the word scratchy in my throat.

She turned to direct our team.

Start, stop, reset. I tested the watch, the plastic slab heavy in my palm. I toed a clump of mud with my boot while I waited for the girls to get ready.

'Go!' Faiza yelled, dropping her orange peel and I started the watch.

Her voice rang like a pistol. The others on the bank raced alongside the peel, which spun as it bobbed, turning like heads…

'Go away!' Faiza had yelled last week in the middle of Geography, and we'd gaped, wondering why she was standing up and glaring at the door.

Mrs Beal, the deputy head, had just knocked and poked her head in, about to ask Miss Rashid something. She also had a beardy bloke in glasses with her, who was waving over her shoulder. But when Mrs Beal saw Faiza's face, she spun around and threw her arms out to bar the way.

'Faiza please, I just want to talk,' said the man, pushing against the door.

'Go away! We don't want you here – GO!'

We looked back and forth, glitter gel pens frozen in our hands.

The man stopped pushing and seemed to notice the rest of the class then, giving us a bleary look from behind his thick glasses. Then, voice cracking, he said, 'Okay, Faiza. Assalamu Alaikum…?' and raised his hand.

But Faiza didn't say, Wa-Alaikum-Salaam. Instead, she said coldly, 'Allah-Hafiz.'

That was the first time I'd heard a man cry. He just sort of crumpled, and let Mrs Beal take him away. Then Miss rushed over to Faiza, who'd started crying too. I already had my packet of tissues in my hand. Just cheap ones from a Poundland multi-pack, but they had Aloe Vera balsam in them and she liked those. But I didn't move. Whispers swept through the room, something about 'dad' and 'kicked out', and then Miss told Nathalie to get tissues from the cupboard and the moment was washed away.

'Stop!' Faiza yelled again now, and I froze the watch.

Beena jogged over with her clipboard and I told her the time. She wrote it down and then went off to tell the others, the pink ribbon on her ponytail flickering in the sharp breeze. I looked down at the stopwatch and pressed reset. The digits blinked back to zeros.

Later, after we'd worked out the average speed, we spread out in a nearby field and emptied our lunch boxes picnic-style on the grass. Miss came around and added an orange from her bag to each one, and soon the air became zingy-sweet as everyone else tore into the fruit. I was sitting with Nat and Beena, half listening to them giggle over who was better looking out of Nick Carter and Justin Timberlake, while I picked grass blades and watched a shaggy brown bull in a neighbouring field. I peeped at Faiza. I wondered if she'd ask Miss for another orange, but she didn't. She looked the same as before, now laughing with Jess. Just like a normal kid. Not like someone with a dad who'd been kicked out of home, who she didn't want to see any more, and who'd tried to catch her at school.

Faiza laughed again, more like a snort, and someone sniggered. I turned around and saw that it was Debbie. She wrinkled her nose, bared her top teeth and jerked her head up and down like a braying horse, and the girls sitting next to her tittered. Then Debbie saw me and stared back. The breeze picked up and there was a whistling in my ears, and then a rushing inside me, like ascending numbers, tens, hundredths of seconds, tripping over each other... and then I felt something reset.

'Stop it,' I said.

Debbie raised her eyebrows. 'What did you say?'

The air prickled between us and more than one extra pair of eyes fell on me, but I held her gaze. 'I said, stop it.'

Debbie's mouth was still open, but I narrowed my eyes, until she muttered darkly and looked away.

Nat and Beena swapped wide-eyes glances, and Faiza didn't even look as if she'd heard. I stared at my hands. They were full of blades of grass, torn and crumpled, but still so green.

'Let's have a race!' said someone else, and everyone seemed to reply.

'What?'

'Yes!'

'No!'

'Come on!'

We looked at Miss Rashid. She checked her watch, then smiled and nodded.

Clearly, all this fresh northern air had gone straight to their heads, 'cause instead of lolling around gossiping, half of the girls actually got up. Jess started them off. 'On your marks...' she began, and they lined up, even Faiza.

And then they were off.

I knew she wouldn't win. Candice was the fastest and she was already in the lead. But I watched Faiza tear off like a mad thing, limbs flailing, caught in the current of sheer distraction. And even though she wouldn't win, I got up this time, to give her my orange when she finished.

THE LEICESTER WRITES SHORT STORY PRIZE 2020

Pancake Day
JUDY BIRKBECK

Blooming cheek! She'd only just moved in and there she was in my seat, sitting with her legs planted apart, scoffing from a bag of fudge all to herself. Butter fudge, my favourite! And how did *she* get fudge, I wonder? I picked up my walking frame and brandished it at the usurper.

'That's my seat.'

She leapt up, glowering.

'Take it then, you barmpot.'

She tried to lift the chair but it toppled to the floor, narrowly missing my toes. Deliberate, I'll bet. The woman next to her moaned in her sleep, her head fallen to one side. The other residents sat in rows round the edge of the room and watched silently.

'Did you see that?' I shrieked at the carer, as they like to call them. Carer my foot! Couldn't care less. Trip you up as soon as look at you, they would. Only no shriek came out, just a croak because of a polyp on a vocal cord. I'd been waiting for surgery God knows how long because the arrogant consultant took issue with me. 'She threw my chair at me.'

'Now, now, ladies.' The so-called carer squeezed the newcomer's shoulder. 'Plenty of seats for everyone. Mrs Bradley-Law particularly likes that chair because of back trouble. There are more in the corner.'

'Why should she sit in the sun and not me?' she said, gripping the bag of fudge as if I might pinch it.

The girl righted the overturned chair and I promptly ensconced myself before that high-and-mighty newcomer could poach it, but she stomped off, chuntering about better company in her own room.

'Everyone knows this is my seat.'

'The new lady has memory problems.' The girl encircled my legs with the walking frame. 'She was very disorientated by the move.'

'Shouldn't steal other people's places, then, should she?'

Mutterings of 'fine welcome' and 'thinks she owns this place' came from the alcove. I ignored them and took a Lion Bar from my handbag, peeled back the wrapper, bit off a chunk and savoured the delicious mix of smooth milk chocolate, chewy caramel and crispy wafer.

The girl gave me a sickly-sweet smile, like some Disney princess with her rosy lips and curly gold locks. Hadn't seen her before either. Trying to soft-soap me. I knew the type: sugar to your face, acid behind your back. A lifetime of teaching taught me that.

Deathly place! Endless fields, not a soul in sight. The most interesting thing seen from my window all afternoon was a hay baler. Hideous brown and beige room. Useless staff: been ringing for ages. Suppose I'd fallen and broken a hip? What then? I'd sue them, that's what. Teach them a lesson.

Why pay all that money to be treated like some naughty seven-year-old? 'I'm not having it,' I muttered to myself.

'Well, Mrs Bradley-Law, you have had a field day, haven't you?'

The girl who'd sided with that newcomer stealing my place the previous day stood in the doorway, didn't even come in, merely looked at the carpet littered with a slew of pill bottles soused in banana syrup as if I'd swiped the lot onto the floor on purpose. I waved my long-handled reacher at her.

'Took your time, didn't you?'

She had a crinkle of a smile at the corner of her lips, I swear, playing games with me like the rest of them, thought they could do what they wanted with us oldies.

'I'll be back.'

That was the last I saw of her for a good half hour, I reckon; probably making overtures to the newcomer or sucking up to matron.

Finally – finally! – she returned with bucket and cloth and started wiping each bottle.

'And who are you?' I barked.

'I'm new. I started yesterday.'

'Cloth-head! What's your name?'

'Christine.'

I fastened my hawk eyes on her every move; these girls didn't bother if they could get away with it. Just flick the cloth over the carpet and leave you in squalor.

'You missed a bit on the square bottle,'

She picked it off the table, examined the cap as if she couldn't see anything, then wiped round it. Humouring me. She needed her eyes testing, that's what. After she'd squeezed out the cloth for the last time I wanted my clothing adjusted. When not bedridden with arthritis, I could walk without assistance but struggled with dressing, being rather overweight. These young whippersnappers had no idea what it was like, unable to reach your toes, stuck in here with only mealtimes to look forward to.

'Do it properly. Tuck my top in.'

She complied, smiling, and watched me hobble to my chair by the window. I studied her face.

'You're not so bad after all, are you? I bet *you*'d not dump your mother in a place like this, nothing to see but grass.'

Not quite true: beyond was a copse with rooks and owls.

She seemed to be waiting. They'd probably warned her I was a mardy cow, but who wouldn't be, trapped here, half the people doolally, the other half stuck up? And she'd be useless if I fell, a mere slip of a lass.

'Why are you here?'

Sounded crusty, I know, but you had to watch some of these people.

'The job was advertised, and I've worked in care homes in my home town.'

'Where's that?' I snapped.

'York.'

'Hm.' I stared, wondering if I could trust this one.

Unless I was bedbound, I always went down to the dining room at noon for dinner. That day it was rubbish: broccoli too crunchy, chicken minimal, cheapskate home trying to compensate with a huge pile of mashed potato. But this girl had pacified me with promises of sticky toffee pudding and ice cream with pieces of fudge in it.

'Fudge?' I'd kill for fudge.

'Homemade, Mrs Bradley-Law. It's sticky, gooey and sweet. And you can have cream as well if you want.'

Her radiant smile put me in mind of some of my sweeter pupils: endearing, chirpy little creatures, do anything for you – run errands, carry books – anything. Bright-eyed, bent on pleasing. My daughter was like that at their age. Not now. Not now, the bitch.

The following afternoon I was staring out of my window. The only excitement was a buzzard with a rabbit in its talons, squealing like air escaping from the pinched neck of a balloon, and I was wondering why I had to wait till six for tea when I was paying all this money, and oddly hoping to see Christine's cheery face and her sunny disposition. Bless her, she had no idea what it was like, imprisoned in an old body.

So imagine my delight when Christine took me out that afternoon – my first time out in months. In the lobby we passed Mrs High-and-Mighty who thought she could sit where she wanted, and it gratified me no end, seeing her green with jealousy. I smiled for a quarter of a mile. We walked along the towpath, or rather, Christine pushed me.

'Let's sit for a bit,' I said, 'so I can see your face.'

All the dog walkers gave us a friendly 'Hallo'. Dogs too, though more likely it was our tutti frutti ice creams in cornets they craved. I wrapped my tongue round the edge and half-closed my lips over the top, savouring the tiny chunks of cherry, raisins and pineapple, and lifted it out of reach of the drooling jaws.

'Any news on your throat operation?'

'No. No chance.' I patted a Labrador. 'I sang solos for the church, you know? I was sought after in those days. Don't get old, Christine. It's not nice getting old.'

She was sympathetic, listened intently, and a yellow wagtail darted up and down the river.

'I feel almost light enough to fly after it,' I joked.

We ambled back to the home, to the sound of rippling water and birdsong, and on the way I bought a bag of delicious melt-in-your-mouth butter fudge which I shared with her. At the door to my room, I cocked my head on one side.

'You're not like the rest of them,' I said, 'stealing and all sorts, and I know what they think of me. But you, you're a treasure, you are.'

She smiled awkwardly.

'Bring me my tea in my room tonight,' I said, excited because this was Pancake Day, the best day of the year.

At six on the dot footsteps approached, a knock, the door opened and Christine breezed in.

'Here we are, Mrs Bradley-Law,' she sang. 'Your tea.'

Then I saw what was on the tray. Horror!

'I never asked for scrambled eggs. You can take them right back.' She stood there gawping. 'Two poached eggs on toast, I said. And mind they're not runny: whites should be white. I can't stand them runny.'

I hurled this last warning at her back. Fifteen whole minutes I had to wait, though admittedly, when she at last arrived, the whites looked perfect. I prodded each one: no clear liquid.

'I made them myself,' she said.

It seemed Christine was not bad at making poached eggs, better than cook, but I kept that opinion to myself.

'Stay and talk to me. Save you running up and down.'

To my surprise she sat down. Anyone else would have said they were busy, but not this one. Charming little lass.

'So tell me, love, what brought you away from York to this neck of the woods?'

She smiled. 'I fancied a change.'

'I do hope you'll not leave like all the rest.'

'Oh no, I want to stay here, if I pass my trial period.'

Most noble, I must say. To be applauded, absolutely. She had altered my rather negative view of the young today, radically. Yes, I can say with assurance, her happy face and selfless attitude had restored my faith in humanity. I chuckled.

'I can't wait for my pancake for pudding. Maple syrup and cream, I'll have.' I swallowed.

'Pancake? Oh no, Mrs Bradley-Law, Shrove Tuesday's tomorrow. It's Monday today.'

My heart plummeted. Such a horrid shock.

'But I've looked forward to it all year.' My lips quivered.

'Only one day to go,' she chirped.

'And I've been thinking about pancakes all day. They're my all-time favourite. It was the one day I looked forward to as a child.'

Ah, the memories... pancakes with lemon juice and oodles of sugar, or thick, sleek chocolate spread, or caramel sauce and peach slices, or the syrup from a jar of stem ginger, but maple syrup and cream were the best.

She patted my hand. I attacked the toast with oozing yolk and gobbled it down to hide my distress.

'I was a teacher all my life, you know,' I said, feeling uneasy under her candid gaze. 'You wouldn't believe it now, but I had a booming voice back then. Seven- and eight-year-olds. Lovely age, do what you want with them. Putty in my hands. My daughter was like that at that age. Not now. Run a mile before she'd do anything to make my life easier. Not that she could run, the size of her.'

She nodded.

'Children these days have no respect. In my day they'd not have dared cross me, but nowadays the little blighters are downright rude.'

She nodded again.

A buzzard flew towards the copse with carrion in its talons.

'What's for pudding today, then?'

'Fruit salad or spotted dick and custard.'

'Spotted dick, please.'

'I'll go and get it now.'

'Thank you, love.'

'My pleasure.'

So obliging. Warms the heart, it does.

'Now then, Mrs Bradley-Law,' I triumphed, bearing the pancake aloft. 'The moment you've waited for all year.'

It was fully dark outside. I'd left most of my beans on toast on the overbed table in anticipation, being assured of a second pancake if I wished. And I certainly would wish. I hauled myself upright on my pillows. She set the tray on the table by the window and sat down herself.

'This looks scrumptious,' she said, looking across.

'Bring it here then.'

To my horror she cut into the pancake and savoured a chunk. What treason was this? She knew I couldn't move from my bed. Saliva dribbled down my chin.

'Mmm. Double cream,' she said with unswerving focus on my face. 'And real maple syrup. Mmmm. None of this imitation stuff.' She carved it into tiny pieces and nibbled slowly on each one.

I grabbed the alarm cord and squeezed the button, repeatedly, but there was no sound.

'I've disconnected it.'

'Help!' I tried to shout, but my voice cracked.

She carried on eating, impassive, making little mm-mm sounds of pleasure. When she had finished, she stood up and rubbed her belly. '*That* was absolutely delicious. Would you like me to get you another pancake, Mrs Bradley-Law?'

I was weeping when she returned with the second one. She didn't care. She was enjoying every moment. And I thought she was so sweet. I wished I'd not left some of the beans on toast.

'But why?'

'Do you not remember? Oh, Mrs Bradley-Law, how could you forget? I come from Selby, not York. I was some of the putty you discarded years ago, the one you always blamed for disappearing pencils and rubbers. I was kicked and pinched regularly, but still your finger pointed at me. And it was two whole terms before you decided I was not the source of the trouble after all. I was the only one to go without a pancake. Remember how you smacked your lips over that pancake in front of me on Shrove Tuesday – *my* pancake? No? Well, why should you remember? It was nothing to you, was it? But to a seven-year-old… That was the day before my mother farmed me out to my grandmother because I reminded her too much of my sister, remember, Mrs Bradley-Law?'

The last mouthful slithered down her throat and she patted her stomach.

'Don't worry, Mrs Bradley-Law. I'm leaving here today.' She stood up with the tray. 'Goodbye, Mrs Bradley-Law. I'll probably be a mardy cow in my dotage too.'

'Bitch,' I shouted at her back. Just like the rest of them.

THE LEICESTER WRITES SHORT STORY PRIZE 2020

The Curd Maker
TANIA BRASSEY

They say that no one makes curd like I do.

Mum and I used to make it for *Seva*. People said she makes such divinely creamy curd because Mum has a big heart. When she first brought us to India we stayed in half of a Portuguese house with a sandpit under a banyan tree. Brat and I commandeered for our cafe and offered the tanned travellers jellies and cakes carved from wet sand; payment was in sea shells. When I got bored of childish things I went to make the real curd from buffalo milk.

My brother and I used to play happily in Goa before our journey to the Ganges. When Mum announced he idea before we left home in Wiltshire I was surprised that she was taking us to India - only to drown Brat in the river. I was sad that he would be left to sink while we threw flower petals. Then it evolved into my favourite daydream. I felt disappointed when he only had a dunk in the muddy river for his seventh birthday with noisy loudspeakers relaying chants from all directions.

By the time we reached this crowded Ashram with its tower blocks wedged between the big river and the fierce ocean I felt sure life would be easier without my brother. He is a show off; always the one to attract attention with his monkey tricks. Now that Mum has gone he's become a pain in the butt. Malawi-Aunty who lives by the elevator says it's because he misses Mum. Then what about me?

Malawi-Aunty asked me an odd question: she said

Did your Mummy make a vow, child? Did she promise to hand you and Krishna to Sadguru?

Does the old bat think Mum has left Krishna and me here forever?

At this ashram which has been our home for the past year no one gets paid for doing *Seva*. The devotees have jobs. Mine is making curd for the International Cafe. That's why we're allowed a free breakfast. They never had a child make the curd before: the pan containing fifty litres of buffalo milk takes two grown-ups to lift off the fire. When overseas devotees tire of the free meals served in aluminium buckets they pay for their fix of comfort food here. We used to come and eat with Mum but now, without money, we rely on our freebie. On weekends we have toast and Bovril with a mug of Milo provided by Malawi-Aunty. We join her on the small piece of terrace where breezes blow off the ocean. Brat waters her plants as she lights camphor on dried coconut shells in a burner 'to purify us'. She cant be sure what germs we may pick up in the village. Incense won't get rid of the nits in my hair so Malawi Aunty is guardian of my scalp.

If I were older they would not allow me to work while having periods. I'm tall for my age so they think I'm a teenager already: Indian devotees unfailingly call out

Its not your time of the month, suuure? Not allowed for kitchen duties, ah?

They repeat this like a mantra each time I start work. I asked Malawi-Aunty -we don't know her real name- why it makes them stressed. She shrugs:

Unclean, no?

What will we do when Malawi-Aunty goes away from May till August when it gets too hot? She owns her apartment for life. When she dies it goes back to the ashram. Mum had to pay the daily rate of 400 Rupees a day for room and food. She paid for us to attend the Hindi school though real Hindu's won't send their children since foreign kids like our Danish and Dutch schoolmates will corrupt them. People cluck their tongues and say Sadguru's plan to unify his Ashram backfired.

Brat has become good at foraging for things people leave behind. We barter milk-shake powder, cooking oil and tooth paste when foreign visitors turn up without supplies. Those who come for a month are the best bet as they leave behind new clothes, shoes and even, a mango wood drum. Indians who arrive at weekends and festival days from Calcutta are the mingy ones. Though they politely call us Young man and Young lady when they ask to take a photo they can't believe we have to fend for ourselves. Last week I helped a lady dressed in a grand sari over the footbridge. In accentless English she asked how long I was staying.

Until we find my mother! She went to do a course. Trapeze....or maybe Taize? We're not sure. We may be here when you visit next year.

After her ferry-boat pulled away I sank down on the muddy jetty and bawled my eyes out. That was the same boat Mum left on. I never cried then because we didn't know; we thought she was only staying two weeks as she had paid Viola to babysit us. I don't believe Mum has left us; she loves us.

I know that for a fact.

I try using the washing lines on Lotus Block rather than our flat roof because it has the best pickings for un-collected laundry! It has sixteen floors so Brown Eagles fly over after sunset. While scrounging shalwar shawls and jeans between the flapping sheets I collide with Viola. In term-time she is one of the serious students at the Vet School, she helps organize our netball. Viola tells me that a visiting Swami has requested to meet Brat and me. So I resort to having my hair plaited by Malawi- Aunty who is gagging to do the monthly delouse. I am not eager to climb into the brown shalwar kameeze that we wear for school. But that's all that fits me now apart from jeans.

Usually 'Tea' here means a metal cup of Marsala chai and a rusk. When we turn up at Eyebright Villa where VIP's stay, I can't believe it: a table cloth, a tea pot, egg sandwiches properly made with mayonnaise, fruit salad from a tin, two laasi's from the Juice Bar are laid out as if for a kids party on a cement garden table. Just as well Brat had showered and jelled his hair back. It was only Viola and us.

How come, Krishna... Viola says stroking my newly dressed plaits, *they don't make you shave your head - like the other boys? You got a great shaped head...*

Because we're not Indian, Brat replies, scoffing his second sarni.

Not Indian at all - echoes a London voice behind us.

A white-robed swami sweeps in and touches my forehead and Krishna's in greeting. The air is filled with the same scent that our Sonya Gran used.

I stare at the white woman with shaved head and holy ash applied more like misplaced make-up. Her deep blue eyes look ringed with purplish kohl.

*Heaven help us, Viola. Not **two** of them?* She is looking from Krishna to me. Her eyebrows are like blond feathers stuck on.

The Swami sits beside us. Viola makes a signal indicating I should *Namaskaar* like we are drilled to do for holy people. I scramble up and yank Krishna to his feet. Swami ruffles his hair and whispers.

No need children since there's nobody but us...

The lady-Swami laughs showing that she has done a good deal of laughing in her life.

Tuck in before the flies descend.

She chats like we are chums on the 49 bus and tells me - as Brat eats for England - that I am the spitting image of my mother.

Did you know, Piyara, Mummy used to bring you to my Yoga class in Wandsworth when you were a tiny baba? You lived in London at the bottom of my road. You were as good as gold but when got to the meditation you'd start grumbling for your feed. Yes, lets finish those sarni's Krishna. I'll be done for if we leave evidence of eggs being cracked in this holy place.

My heart does a leap.

She knows our Mum, I mouth to Brat. She knows us!

After tea Viola heads off for *satsang*. Who needs classes in wisdom when we have refills of pomegranate laasi today? Its nice to sit under the Ganeesha tree till the sound of chanting from the naff new temple drowns the mosquito humming. Swami says she was so sad to lose contact with Mum after she got ordained and left Wandsworth for Bihar. She talks about many daughters and sons, one of whom, Kim - was my only babysitter because Mum didn't trust anyone else with *the dear tiny thing you were.*

It is comforting to talk to someone who has known Mum as a friend and knew me as a *'tiny thing'*. Swami Lalleshwari is not like the random strangers who have tried to adopt Krishna and me during their India stay. When the Scots couple took us to Tamil Nadu for *Holi,* Brat followed him like a puppy, mimicking the Glaswegian accent. Last week I reminded Krishna about those to but he couldn't even remember them! I envy his ability to blank people from his memory so that he cannot be sad about them leaving. Or about our predicament. That is the word our Swami friend used. She's cross that Sadguru has let us be stranded here but says she's walking on eggshells. I think I know what she means. She doesn't want to make things awkward for Mum when she returns.

The evening that Swami-Ji leaves for Bihar we go to prayers after Bhajans. Swami-Ji puts blessed ash on our forehead and gives me a mantra which I'm forbidden to tell anyone else. Swami wants to find a way of joining us with our Mum.
Yes Swami-Ji. I'd really like you to.
She holds my gaze and nods gravely, *I know you do, my love.*
Krish tries to copy me. But instead he blurts out
Yes-thank-you-Mum. But-don't-ever-leave-us--because-I-love-you-Mummy!
He blurts it so fast that Swami doesn't realize its like a prayer for Mum. Or did the moron imagine Swami Lalleshwari was our Mum come back with blue eyes?

Swami-Ji does not laugh: her eyes fill up as she walks us through the crowd. Putting a hand on our shoulders, she forces a path through the temple where people are chanting, waiting, praying. We get clear of the stifling, incense-soaked air to where the sun has set leaving a *seenimuthu* pink sky. I'm aware that our Swami friend grows taller like a magic genie each time we see her. She clasps workmanlike hands on my shoulder and on Krishna, leads us to the two cupolas and turns us round so we face the *Vimana* while she faces outward to the fierce, unruly waves.

Then my ears stop hearing the words she's saying. Her mouth is moving but no sound: I shake my fingers in my ears and my hearing clears. In a much softer voice she seems to be talking to herself...

.... are special children. Very blessed young people. Perhaps the reason you were sent here is not clear to you now. One day when you are far from here - and you WILL be, dudes. You'll know it was some kind of training - you know Krishna, like your training with Footy? Don't take this as a punishment. Its simply a process. Understand?

A shiver runs down my body. Swami holds our chins up so we gaze into the ocean of her eyes.

Yes, loud and clear! pipes Brat in a voice of some cartoon character.

My throat locks. I'm so afraid that any minute I might burst into sobs. I can't believe that Swami is about to leave us and we can't do anything to stop her.

From a woven purse Swami extracts a leaf and pops it under my tongue; she does the same with Brat saying

Don't chew it, it's Holy Tulsi.

A temple Swami in brown robes appears with some ashram high and mighty. They seem scared our Swami may not want to leave us and briskly usher her to a car in the sandy courtyard where chapels are left. A crowd of women are draping long garlands of marigolds over it like they do for wedding cars. Seeing that familiar white Oxford Ambassador waiting to take our friend the only one to connect us to Mum - makes me want to hide in the boot and escape with her. I'm sure the same thought has occurred to my brother.

Swami descends the steps in bare feet followed by a worried gaggle of Brahmacharyni in flimsy white sari's, as if ready to catch a bride's bouquet. Swami-Ji slides easily into the marigold-festooned car and winds down the window.

I try to move. To catch her eye. To wave. Neither my brother nor I can leave the spot. Maybe Swami-Ji has turned us invisible with the leaf she put in our mouth? Or is it the effect of the Mantra? I can't understand why here by the Indian Ocean so far from home – where Mum grew cauliflowers and broad beans for the Corsley Show - I don't feel abandoned any longer. Yet I am welded to this floor.

I'm not sure how long I can keep my Mantra a secret. Or how to stop myself from strangling Brat, but I know one thing. I will not let on how I make my curd so creamy.

THE LEICESTER WRITES SHORT STORY PRIZE 2020

Mooly
J. R. MCMENEMIE

Put your hand onto the window, and look at your reflection. Can you see? You look like an angel. An angel in the darkness, that's what you are. Can you see behind the image of yourself on the glass? Good, you're really looking now, you have to squint a little bit but you can see it. It's bright, isn't it? Glowing above your reflection like a halo. The halo of a beautiful angel. Don't move, don't let them see you. Just stand by the window with the others, looking out. Isn't it pretty? They told you not to look, to keep away from the windows, but they don't know anything. Mooly told you not to listen to them. Mooly always said they were stupid.

Can you see where you live? Don't worry if you can't. It's quite far away now, and the light shining from the cracks is very bright. You can remember what the house looked like though, can't you? White painted wooden boards and big heavy doors that you had to push hard to open. Do you remember playing teasets on the lawn in the summer, you and Mooly? You must've been about 4 years old, and you had that lovely collection of wooden teacups and saucers, a little teapot with little wooden teabags. It was a fantastic set. There was even a wooden cake that had tiny wooden strawberries. You used to drop them into the pot instead of the bags, and say "strawberry tea" and Mooly would laugh and say how silly you were.

You loved playing with Mooly. You asked Mummy and Daddy if Mooly could come for tea once, but they made that face, you know, the secret screwy up one they do to each other that they think you don't notice. But you did notice, and when you told Mooly that they'd said no, it upset him and you had to sit with him all night, saying how angry you were at Mummy and Daddy, that they didn't understand Mooly was your best ever friend.

You can hear people crying behind you, but you mustn't be scared, just stay by the window. Mooly told you not to be frightened. He said some people would be very upset but you had to be strong, and one day you'll realise that it was a happy thing that happened and not sad at all. Look at the cracks now, so bright, one is really big and wide, it looks like when you tear out a piece of an orange. You like oranges. There was an orange tree in your garden. Daddy planted it when you were born and called it "Lucy's tree" and said that all the oranges it grew belonged to you. Do you remember when you and Mooly decided to make orange juice and pulled all the oranges off the tree? Daddy was very angry about that. You said that they were your oranges and you could do what you liked with them, but Daddy said something about keeping things safe for the future. That made Mooly giggle and so you started laughing too, and Daddy's face went red and he got angry. He asked you if Mooly had told you to pull the oranges off the tree and you said yes, and Daddy said that he didn't want you playing with

Mooly anymore, and it was about time that Mooly went away and left you alone. Mooly really didn't like that idea because you were his best friend ever, and he said he was going to make sure that you would never be separated, no matter what Daddy said.

Mummy and Daddy took you to see a doctor called Doctor Allman. You didn't like him did you? He smelt of burnt newspaper and looked very worried all the time. He asked you lots of questions about Mooly, like if he'd ever asked you to do things you didn't feel were right, and you said "like Uncle Peter?" And Dr Allman said no, and didn't ask you any questions at all about Uncle Peter. He sent you to the big hospital, where they made you wear a horrible paper dress and stuck pins in you. They hurt you and put you in a big machine that made scary noises and you cried. Mooly watched you crying through the window and it made him very upset. He didn't know why they were hurting you so much until he heard Daddy tell Mummy that this was going to make Mooly go away, and Mooly got scared. That was when the first crack appeared, in a place called Iceland, which Daddy said was very far away so you shouldn't get too upset about it. You told Mooly about it but he didn't say anything.

Daddy worked in the big science building. He was very important. When you came out of hospital, he brought you a big spaceship with wheels on that you could pedal around the garden. He said some of his friends had made it for you, and you could pedal to anywhere you want. You said you wanted to pedal to Mooly's house. Daddy shouted at you to "stop talking about bloody Mooly!" And made you cry. Daddy said that Mooly wasn't real, but you cried and stomped around and shouted at Daddy that Mooly was real and he was your best friend ever. Daddy told you it was a load of rubbish, and that you couldn't go to Mooly's house because you didn't know where it was, so that night when Mooly came to visit, you asked him.

Mooly tried to tell you where his house was, but you couldn't remember, there were so many turns, it was very complicated and difficult to understand, so Mooly told you to write it down and show it to Daddy, because Mooly really wanted you to visit him. When you showed Daddy where Mooly's house was, Daddy gave you a funny look and went very quiet. He asked you all kinds of questions about Mooly, like how long he'd been visiting you, and what you did with him. You told the truth and said you'd known Mooly since you were a baby, and you played together, he was your best ever friend. Daddy told you to tell him the next time Mooly came to visit, because he had some important things to ask him, but Mooly was still upset with Mummy and Daddy for not letting him come for tea, and he didn't want to talk to anybody else but you. He said he was angry with Daddy for not believing he was real, but if Daddy said sorry then Mooly would show him how to get to Mooly's house.

After that, Daddy didn't want to split you and Mooly up anymore. He asked lots of questions about the things you did together, and had other things written in a pad that you were told to show Mooly when he visited. But when Mooly came to visit that night, he didn't want to answer any of Daddy's questions and you played "show dancers" instead, each taking it in turn to hide behind the curtains and then burst out with a routine for the other one.

Mooly wasn't a good dancer. You were better, because you'd had lessons, and you tried to teach Mooly how to do a pirouette, but you tripped on a piece of railway and fell into the window. You banged your head and it hurt, and you were very upset and you cried. But Mooly kissed your head and it all went away. You had a small lump for a few days but it didn't hurt anymore. Mummy asked you how you got it. You said you'd been dancing with Mooly and had slipped. Mummy was very angry and told Daddy to take you back to the hospital, but Daddy said no, and they shouted at each other until Daddy whispered something to Mummy and she went very quiet, and they both looked at you in a way you'd never seen them look at you before. But Mummy still didn't want you to play with Mooly. She said she was scared for you, and wanted Mooly to go away. So she took you to the hospital without Daddy knowing and Dr Allman put pins in you again and you cried, and Mooly was very angry, and he remembered saying he was never going to let them split you up, and he shouted at Mummy, but she didn't hear him.

Turn around. Can you see them there? Mummy and Daddy are holding hands and looking at you in the same way. Mummy has been crying, her eye makeup has gone all smudgy and her hair is fluffed up. Daddy's holding the picture that Mooly drew for him, the squiggly one.

Do you remember it? That night Mooly came to visit and you did painting and drawing. You drew a big volcano gushing bright red lava into a blue sea. You'd seen it on the TV, a man who looked worried like Dr Allman, said that an island had been broken in half by a big volcano, and you drew it later for Mooly.

Mooly just drew boxes and squiggles. You told him how funny it looked, but Mooly was very quiet that night and told you to just show it all to Daddy in the morning, and that he couldn't come to visit you for a while. You got upset and asked Mooly why he couldn't come anymore, but he said he couldn't tell you.

When Daddy saw the pictures, he had to sit down, and he said "did Mooly draw these?" And you said yes, and Daddy said some rude words like the ones Uncle Peter used to say, and his face went all worried like the man on the TV.

Mooly didn't visit again for weeks. When he came back, you cried and told him how lonely you'd been and how much you'd missed him. Mooly said he was sorry for being away, and for shouting at Mummy. Mooly was very sorry. He told you that when he gets angry at things he sometimes shouts, and he doesn't mean to but sometimes he can't control it. He said that sometimes when he shouts, it can be very loud in a way that can wobble things. He was very sorry for leaving you alone, for so long, but he'd had to go somewhere else for a while. He said he was sorry for making things wobble, and to tell Mummy he was sorry for shouting, but Mummy pulled a face and said she wasn't interested and told you to stop it. You didn't know what she meant, but Mooly did. Mooly knew that Mummy thought you were making it all up, and that made Mooly angry again.

Keep looking through the window, outside, at the Earth. It looks a bit like an egg, a cracked egg, all the yolk running out like when you and Mooly made cakes, and Mummy walked in and shouted at you for making such a mess. Grown ups are stupid. Mooly always said they were stupid. If they'd left us alone, then Mooly wouldn't have got angry, and the cracks wouldn't have appeared, and Mooly wouldn't have had to explain to Daddy and his friends how to get to Mooly's house. But they are stupid, and they are angry at things they don't believe are real. They dont make any sense. Mooly is sorry for the people who were left behind. He didn't mean to hurt them, Lucy, but when he gets angry it makes things wobble. Mooly is very sorry for making things wobble. He's sorry for the cracks, and that you had to leave your house. He's sorry for making the Earth look like a broken egg, but you can all come and live with Mooly now. Uncle Peter can't come though. Mooly did something to Uncle Peter's car, and Uncle Peter is too poorly to come.

If you keep looking out, past the reflection and the halo and the bright deep lines in the surface of the Earth, can you see all the little white dots floating around? They are the other people in their spaceships, they all live in space now too, on their ships that Daddy helped to make. Look out past them. Follow the big crack on the right side of Earth all the way down, until you reach the bottom. Now, can you imagine the same line carrying on, like a spider hanging on a thread all the way into space? Can you see the first star it reaches? That's it. Now look at the star to the left of that one, the little one.

They're going to point all the spaceships at that little star, and in a year you'll be 8, and you'll all have arrived at Mooly's house, and there isn't just Mooly waiting for you, Lucy, but lots of Moolys, all waiting for their new special friends to stay with them. Mooly loves you, Lucy. Look at how beautiful the Earth is, with its bright middle like an egg. It sits above your reflection like a halo on an angel. You are a beautiful angel in the darkness, Lucy, and when you arrive, you'll be with Mooly forever and ever, and no one will be upset or say bad things about it, because they'll all have their own Moolys too.

THE LEICESTER WRITES SHORT STORY PRIZE 2020

Black and White Blues
RICHARD HOOTON

I STARE at the dark mark emerging on my arm from where I caught it against the worktop while getting breakfast, and curse myself for being so clumsy.

'You bruise like a peach,' hubby always tells me.

Something about my pale skins' slow discolouration fascinates me. That's how it is, I think. Always deep down, never immediately apparent, everything appearing normal so that no-one would even know something's wrong. But slowly it surfaces until it's all too obvious.

Still in my PJs, I sink into our battered old sofa, unsure of whether I'm sluggish or leisurely. A mug of black coffee cools on the glass-top table. Alongside, remnants of muesli congeal in a bowl.

I flick through the TV channels – to be honest, I preferred it when there was less choice and I only really put it on to fill the room with noise and motion – then settle on something familiar. Phil is in a black tie dinner suit with Holly wearing a flowing white gown, not the usual getup for morning telly. They say something about having gone straight to the studio after an awards ceremony; they've not been home, their night merging into day. They move to the studio kitchen, chatting amiably about the perils of making homemade soup. While it's not exactly profound, I'm struggling to follow the thread, to take it all in. My eyelids feels as heavy as trapdoors, my brain unwilling to ignite.

Then Phil says: 'Oh! I've never whizzed it all over the kitchen.'

Holly's jaw drops. Phil's face mirrors hers as he realises what he's said. Mischievous grins stretch and they're off, laughter rippling through them, a tide rising into a tsunami.

Eventually, they manage to control themselves.

'Ooh, we haven't done this for a long time,' says Holly.

She's referring to their tendency to corpse, but it sets them off again, collapsing into fits of giggles. It spreads infectiously around the studio.

But it doesn't reach me.

Normally, I'd be shaking with laughter too. Something's wrong though, something that I can't quite put my finger on. I stare at the screen, the unsettled feeling intensifying. Phil's salt and pepper hair's the same but Holly's lost her usual bounce, her hair bleached and face pallid, a Snow White figure. The set is similarly shaded and that's when the penny drops: our 50inch Ultra HD flat screen has regressed to black and white.

I stand and thump the side of the TV as if it's an old cathode ray tube I can spark back into life. It doesn't make the blindest difference.

Then I notice the rest of the lounge.

My stomach turns with the realisation.

It's not just the TV.

It's everywhere.

There's not a drop of colour, not even a pigment, to enhance the room; as if it's become a 1950s broadcast.

'Stop it,' cackles Holly.

'I can't,' weeps Phil.

I turn them off.

I slam the trapdoors shut, retreating into the cover behind my eyelids. Rub crusts of sleep from the creases around them. Tell myself it's just vision adjusting to light. Count to a slow ten. Haul them back open.

The room's still chequered.

I stand in silence. It's broken by a sharp knocking. I wonder who is outside and what they want but I can't open the door like this, dressed in my pyjamas at mid-morning and all shaky.

The noise again. Insistent. The letterbox jangles.

'Mrs Palmer.' The gravelly voice of our window cleaner. 'It's just Gary. Collecting my rounds.'

I move into the hallway.

'Mrs Palmer? Are you in?'

I daren't open the door. I fear what's out there. Is everything affected? Has colour bled from the whole wide world?

The letterbox rattles shut. Footsteps scuff the garden path, growing fainter until gone.

I scale the stairs and enter my bedroom. The ceiling's a night sky without stars, the walls a blank void, my wardrobe a dark presence in the corner. Butterflies in the motif above the bookcase are now moths.

I crawl under the duvet, once lilac, now jet, and huddle into a ball. My body feels somehow both drained and a lead weight. Perhaps if I close my eyes I'll drift off to sleep and when I awake everything will be fine.

Dreams don't come. Just a restless gloom.

I look at my alarm clock. It blinks 11:00, its white digits falling into a black hole screen. Morning has leaked away with the colour. Vague notions of contacting someone mist my mind. I can't disturb him. Not again. Who else will understand?

It's stale and stuffy in here. I want to open a window but don't have the courage. Snatches of activity outside spill into the room: rumbling wheels, a dog barking in the distance, muffled ghostly voices here and there.

The world is carrying on as normal.

As reluctant as I am, I'll have to see for myself.

Freeing an arm from the duvet's trappings, I tug it to one side, lumber from the bed and shuffle past a shadowy chest of drawers, reaching out to curtains draped like a wedding dress.

I hold my breath and feel my heart stammering inside my ribcage as if a condemned prisoner. I hesitate. Then yank the curtains wide.

A monochrome world lies before me. Summer's become winter, my heart freezing with it. An icy sheen glistens on the road, the buildings behind a pencil sketch on an empty page, the landscape beyond similarly untouched by the artist's paints. It could seem scenic or even nostalgic. But I ache for the beauty of colours, their vibrancy and depth, to return.

Falling back onto the bed, I gaze at midnight before finally deciding that, however daunting, I have to venture outside and face this strange world. I wriggle tight jeans over pyjama bottoms then wrestle into a sweater and leather jacket. Catching a glimpse in the mirror of a goth-like figure, I leave the bedroom and trudge down a lace staircase, fearing that it won't support my weight. As I reach the front door a voice tells me not to risk it. In a rare moment of defiance, I step outside.

Above hangs a slate sky strewn with cotton wool wisps, the sun now a moon. Treading carefully, so as not to slide on frosted slabs, I pull the jacket tight around me as coldness prickles exposed skin.

All the birds are ravens who've escaped the tower to perch on charcoal rooftops. Cawing, they have no songs, only stares. Keeping my head down I avoid cracks in the ice that might swallow me.

'Oi, watch where you're going!'

Whoever I almost walked into skirts around me. I don't look up.

The outdoor market nears. Once upon a time, I loved browsing amid the hustle and bustle. It's the best thing about where we live: the chance, just moments from our doorstep, to savour the smell of cinnamon and cardamom, to soak up the sight of roses and carnations, to discover an unknown treasure or keepsake.

As I near, a deadweight in my stomach tells me something's changed. The buzz of chatter and waves of movement are missing. Just the odd figure lists down a murky walkway and the rainbow striped canvases are washed-out.

'Get your apples and pears.' A lone voice bellows through the barrenness. 'Spuds, one pound a kilo.'

I reach the flower stall. Petals bereft of hue droop over pale stalks like snowdrops. Sullied ones curl inwards over rotted stigma. Others mix the contrast, resembling dark geraniums whose black centres cascade towards a white fringe as if ink's been spilt onto blotting paper.

I turn to another stall. Grab an object. It should be vibrant, not the pitted piece of moon rock clutched in my hand. I let it fall and pick up another. Instead of shiny red and green, it's a giant pearl blemished by swirls of soot.

'You alright, love?'

A man with thickset eyebrows and pursed lips stares at me. With his contrasting cap, long-sleeved t-shirt and apron, he resembles a penguin in Antarctica.

What can I say? I just grimace at the boulder in my hand.

'Yer wanna buy anything or just hold 'em?'

It's as if the wintriness has seeped through my skin and into my bones to transform me into an ice sculpture. My tongue is frozen, my glare glacial.

He readjusts some pebbles. Rustles a pile of paper bags. Then pauses as if he's discovered an original thought.

'Cheer up, love. It might never happen.'

Something inside sparks and gushes through my veins to release me. Makes me want to throw the apple at his stupid fucking face. To squeeze the orange until pips burst free from pulp mushed inside my fist and juice as sticky as blood drips down my arm.

His eyes darken. Nose twitches. Grotesque lips mouth other words. The awnings billow and bulge in a vicious gale, a white flag about to be torn apart under a pitch-black sky.

I spin and run.

Away from sneers and stones. From darkness and decay.

Praying that I don't slip and tumble, I vault oily patches and avoid spectral figures. A witch's cat crosses my path, arching its back and hissing as I stumble around it. I daren't stop until the front door is slammed shut, the stairs climbed and I'm back inside my bedroom.

My sanctuary has altered even further in my absence. The ceiling seems lower. The walls narrower. The door smaller. Everything remains colourless.

On the bookshelf is a snow globe, a childhood memento that's somehow remained steadfast amongst changing possessions. It contains a tiny snowman in a permanent Christmas, with lumps of coal for eyes, nose and mouth arranged in a fixed expression. From the age of seven, I have longed to touch him, to know how he feels underneath the cold glass. Thirty years on, I resist the urge to throw it against the wall and set him free.

I retreat back into bed, submerged beneath the duvet where it's warm and calm. I lie there for what must be hours, in the state between sleep and consciousness, never quite at rest but not alert.

Then a key clinks in a lock. I hear the creak of the front door opening. Movement echoes in the lounge below. Footsteps disturb the stairs. A head peers around the bedroom door.

'What's up?'

Concern infuses his voice. But he isn't shaken by what's around him. He mustn't be able to see what I see.

It's not the world that's wrong. It's me.

He crouches next to the bed. 'What is it?'

I squint at him. How can I explain it without men in white coats turning up to take me away?

'Everything's wrong.'

He reaches out and strokes my head, his fingers warm and soft.

'It'll be alright.'

'It's worse than ever.' How can I tell him that this time it's stolen all the colour from my life?

An anxious expression crumples his face. Then something in his eyes startles me. His irises are a milk chocolate brown between the whites and the pupil, as if cream has blended into coffee. They transfix me.

'Come on, lazy head.' He gives my arm a gentle tug. 'Out of bed.'

He stands up and loosens his tie, unfurling it from his shirt collar.

'It's nice out.' Not from my experience. 'Let's go for a walk while it's still light. The fresh air and exercise will do us good.'

Part of me shrivels at the thought of stepping outside again, of wandering back into the cold and dark. But another part, almost lost deep down, reaches up.

'Just for a short while.' He pulls at me again, as if a child with a reluctant pet on a lead. 'For me.'

I obey, clambering out of bed still wearing my jacket.

'Well, there's no need for you to get dressed then.' He laughs but it sounds like metal rattling inside porcelain. 'That'll save time.'

I follow him downstairs. I have everything I want here – but what does it matter?

He halts in the hallway. 'You taken your pill today?'

I shake my head. He disappears into the kitchen. Returns with a glass and what looks like a sweetener. Gives them to me as if they're presents. I swallow the pill with a gulp of water. He takes my hand, smiles and we step outside. I keep my head down.

'This way.'

He leads me in a different direction to before. Down a side street that takes us to the towpath. After a few minutes we stop.

'Look,' he says. 'In the canal.'

There's another ice sculpture. This time a heron, half-submerged in the water. It's long, thin shape remains so elegantly still that for a moment I think it's not real. An ebony tuft streaks along its head to the curve of its ivory neck. Below them are grey feathers, as if its palette has merged. I watch the heron's stubborn stance but it's the grey that fascinates me.

Suddenly, it snaps free. Dives under the surface. Emerges in a splash with a small fish wriggling in its beak. Wings spread wide, slap air and it flies away.

'You'll get through this. Trust me.' That's easy for him to say, happy with his nine to five and comfortable existence. 'You'll be able to get back to your studies.' My heart drops. I associate that word with loneliness.

We continue our journey, trying not to get bogged down in the muddy pathway. My breathing quickens as our surroundings develop. Silver birch trees give way to umber trunks and russet and amber leaves. An emerald grass mixes with ferns and moss. On a branch, a brightly clothed robin warbles a bittersweet song. For a second, I'm bedazzled by a multi-coloured world.

'This way.' Adam leads me from the canal path back to streets of honey-coloured stone buildings. A golden sun has returned to an azure sky. 'Let's stop at the market to get something for tea.'

I flinch, pull up, and loosen my grip on him. He holds my hand firm, gives it a squeeze and guides me forward. The market's now a cacophony of noise as traders pack away crimson clothes and bronze bound books. I let go of Adam's hand to stand in front of the flower stall. Daffodils and fuchsias and violets blaze with colour. Velvet petals switch from indigo to magenta to blonde. The bulbous heads of tulips shine from ruby to rouge to lemon. I'm mesmerised by shades and tones until Adam's voice breaks the spell. He's at the fruit and veg stall calling me over, a small punnet in each hand.

'For dessert,' he says. 'Strawberries or raspberries?'

I wander over and stare at baskets of brightness, a vivid array of apricots, blueberries, carrots, cherries, limes, pears, peaches and plums. Holding an apple to the light, I revolve it as if it's a planet so that rosy red gives way to a soft jade like continents disappearing into sea.

'Have it if you want. On the house.' I look across to see the stallholder nodding at me. 'Anything to put a smile on yer face.'

I bite into the crisp flesh and its tang fizzes on my tongue, a squirt of juice dribbling down my chin. I laugh, blush and wipe it away with the back of my hand. As he takes Adam's payment, the trader laughs too.

'That's better,' he says.

I eat the rest of the apple as we stroll home, until just a browning core is left. Adam's straight in the kitchen, a clatter of pots and pans. I head for the bedroom, easing open the door with trembling fingers.

I'm struck by the intense beauty of bold butterfly wings. Patches of scarlet melt into an orange as fierce as a tiger's stripe and splashes of ocean deep navy fade to cobalt then teal. I want to grab the colours, hold them close to me, never be without them again.

Something sizzles in the kitchen and the aroma of ginger and mint makes my mouth water. As my stomach rumbles, I realise I missed lunch.

Adam bounds up the stairs. 'You hungry?'

'Famished.'

'Not sure you'll like the food, though.'

'It'll be OK,' I say. 'Just so long as it's not burnt.'

I run my hand over his butterscotch shirt that's so fresh I expect the fabric to ooze over my fingertips.

'And make sure you don't whizz it all over the kitchen.'

Bemusement arises on his face. I stifle a snigger, then let it go, laughing more and more until I can feel it filling my chest and vibrating through my body, the release almost euphoric.

He smiles. 'You seem better, Rachel.'

The laughter leaves me, my body calming.

Then that cold dread is back. Tomorrow could be worse; the colour could go and never return. Like Charlie Chaplin, I'd be forever captured in black and white.

He sees it in my face and shakes his head.

'You'll get better.' There's a defiance in his voice. 'You've just got to stick to your medication. And your counselling starts tomorrow.'

I want to believe him. But I know it's not that easy. That winter always returns.

'I'm here for you.' He kisses me. Makes me feel brighter, bolder, as if the colour comes from inside me.

Whispering three special words in my ear, he envelopes me in a hug. And we hold as tight as a knot, reminding me of our wedding vows.

THE LEICESTER WRITES SHORT STORY PRIZE 2020

Continental Breakfast
ED BARNFIELD

He's gone, but I still feel his hand guiding me at the buffet. The woman in front is amassing an orca-sized portion of smoked salmon, but I hold back, settling for cucumber slices, goat cheese and a wheat thin.

As I pour my orange juice, I notice how much the queue has grown in the last ten minutes; testimony to the superabundance of meats, I suppose, but also a sign of how much this hotel has changed in recent years. Back in the day, the spartan tables of beautiful guests were outnumbered by waiting staff, with a strict choice between kippers, full English or continental. Now, there's a lush savanna of food, mixed with all the bustling atmosphere of a railway platform.

I'm not sure where the impulse to return to 'The Hetton' came from. I suppose I was thinking about my first assignation with Tony, wondering what the place looked like now. When we were young, the hotel offered the luxuries of starched linens and immaculate manners, afternoon sandwiches, and drinks served with excessive formality. He ordered a hamburger in the little cubbyhole behind the bar, and it arrived under a shining steel dome with fat chips like railways sleepers. I was allowed to have one.

'You need to keep your figure for ballet school,' he joked, reminding me of the long-ago lessons of my youth.

I certainly couldn't face Christmas at home this year. The thought of the same people dropping by, wearing the same funeral expressions – the cards following so close on from the condolences. Unbearable.

There were practical considerations, too. I need to complete the awful bureaucracy of mortality, trailing validated copies of Tony's death certificate around banks and such. The architecture firm that bears our name needs to be wound up, and better to do that now rather than wait for the New Year. The hotel's distance and trustworthy wi-fi are helpful in that regard.

'Have you stayed here before?' the receptionist asked, as she reached through the tinsel for my passport, and I fought down the urge to take her back with me, talk about The Hetton I knew thirty years ago, feeling the tremors as the dam inside began to crack. In the event, she was trying to sign me up for corporate membership.

It's really only on the first morning that I scan the faces of anyone beyond the serving staff. Most of the groups here are families from far-flung places around the world; Indians, Arabs and a sprinkling of Chinese. It makes sense, given the geography, the proximity of certain embassies and the tourist draws of the Palace and Hyde Park. Still, I can't help but wonder what Tony would make of it. Here in the breakfast room, everyone – waiters, maître de, guests – is from somewhere else.

I like to think he would have laughed and chided me for my parochialism. Tony had a gift for friendly observation, a fascination for the dramas that spark and spread in our peripheral vision.

'You never know what people around you are going through,' he used to say. 'Unless you speak to them, you can't tell if your neighbour is in crisis or triumph.'

Here at breakfast, I'm surrounded by crisis and triumph. There's an American couple who clearly fought the night before, ordering drinks in the manner of prison guards' testimony. They read news from home on their phones to avoid talking to each other.

I also keep an eye on the Japanese parents, whose daughter refuses to eat. All the maternal cajoling in the world can't get the little girl to lift her head, try a spoonful, while Dad, resolute, reads his newspaper. It's only when they both go back to the buffet that I see the fat young son lean over and spit, quite deliberately, into his sibling's oatmeal. Someone really ought to say something.

The Arabs, I enjoy more. It is a much larger group, who invariably have difficulty being seated together. There are three women of approximately the same age, loud and gossipy, and the source of much speculation among the staff. There are also at least seven children – possibly more – ranging from toddlers up to sullen teens. I like the look of the patriarch, who has a tidy beard, and who is constantly looking over at his brood with little smiles as they argue and scold. His eldest daughter, who covers her hair with a black couture cap, slices fruit for her brother and sisters, tells them to sit straight.

It's nice to be surrounded by such an assortment of other people's families, reminders of the lives you could have had.

My experiment in voyeurism is interrupted by another offer of coffee, and a scent from yesteryear. A basket of steaming pastry is carried past my table with the solemnity of the Sunday service. The Hetton's kitchen used to claim it produced the best croissants in London, at a time when that was still a mark of distinction. Clearly, the new owners have maintained this tradition.

I'm finding that a lot during my stay. The elements I remember are present, but they've been laminated. They handed me a drinks menu on the first night, complete with thumbnail descriptions of each cocktail and the famous guests who may – may – have drunk them in the past.

Still, the croissants smell divine. I take one, wincing as the butter burns my fingertips. No Tony to make remarks about carbohydrates now.

As well as the business, I need to do some social accounting while I'm here. Make a list of the people I can still count on. The nephew and nieces were all Tony's, along with the majority of the friends and business associates. I imagine the funeral is the last time I'll hear from them, unless there's some unseemly scrabbling over the will.

Enough of that. Think about the future. I finish my coffee and pretend to myself that I'm leaving but take a last pass at the bread counter. My hand reaches into the croissant basket, but it's empty. The whole mountain of delicacies gone in the time it takes to eat one. A sign of the times, I suppose. One of the sullen Americans complains to a passing waiter and is told he'll need to wait for 15 minutes for the next batch.

'Not quite the same as Burger King,' I smile, and he looks at me blankly through his Buddy Holly glasses.

My morning is devoted to walking. London buildings always have those interesting crenulations that make looking up worthwhile, like a coat of chiselled history. Still, a lot has changed at ground level. The population seems almost entirely transient and the retail outlets have adapted accordingly, helpful currency converters in every window. The only echo of England I can find is a queue of taxi drivers laughing in the cold.

The afternoon requires more exertion. At home, surrounded by his detritus, it's impossible to separate my view the business from my memories of Tony. I find scribbled notes in his spidery hand and I stop and run my fingers over the indentations, keep stumbling upon signs from an unfinished life in every invoice.

In the hotel, framed by the enormous desk, it's a lot easier to see the red in the ledger. Our company is running enormous debts, late payments and missed deliveries putting almost everything at risk. Soberingly, a lot of the names in the debit column I recognise from the funeral. Rory, who grasped my hand at the hospital and told me what a 'great guy' Tony was, hasn't paid for the barn conversion of three years ago. Alexander, Tony's nephew, has several undeclared loans from us.

That was the way it was with Tony, who came from wealth and always considered himself wealthy, irrespective of how much there actually was in the bank. Debt was just another form of liquidity, he'd say. There was always some scheme in play to ensure the lights stayed on at the end of the month.

Perhaps that's what all this was – another grand plan, cut short by cardiac arrest. Or perhaps he ran out of options and the stress got to him. Either way, it's dismal that I can only learn the precariousness of our position from him now.

I'm musing on this, the unfairness, over breakfast the next day. I know what will happen when I start to chase these debts. Plausible liars like Rory will look pained and say, 'Tony and I had an agreement, didn't he tell you?'

I will have to pause, consider the possibility. Then unkind gossip will filter back to me, the avaricious widow chasing his friends and loved ones for cash.

'You'd have thought he'd left her comfortable enough,' they'll say.

The Americans are back in their customary place, not talking. She is strikingly attractive in comparison to her partner and seems to be the only one still trying to stir up conversation. The bullying continues on the table to my left, the brother whispering what I assume are insults in Japanese just out of his parents' earshot. He licks his finger and stabs it in his sister's grapefruit.

Even my Arab friends are a disappointment. I go for my customary croissant to find another empty basket, another apologetic waiter. On my way back, I notice a whole plate sitting untouched on their table. Someone, probably the daughter, is collecting them every time there's a refill, placing them as a display at the centre of their table next to the sliced fruit.

That sense of entitlement is universal these days. If something is on offer, get your money's worth. Don't think about the people behind you in the queue, the poor pâtissier rolling and folding to feed your endless appetite.

'Take it. It's paid for,' Tony would say to guests, particularly in places like this, where all-inclusive packages could masquerade as examples of his largesse. He was a great drink re-filler, a gleeful opportunist, always encouraging the ladies to have something from the sweet trolley. Well, the other ladies, at least.

It's only now, musing on the unpaid bills and lost invoices, that I can see how they took him at his word – Rory, Alexander, all of the nephews. They took until there was nothing left.

As I'm leaving, I pass the big family's table. One of the women is upset and the man is doing his best to console her, rubbing her hand and speaking in hushed tones. The plate of croissants sits there, cold and uneaten. I shoot what I hope is an unfriendly glare at the daughter, but her head is down, looking at a green newspaper with Arabic script, pointing at a photo.

The next day is December 25th. As I dress, it occurs to me that I have nothing to do for two whole days. No presents to open, no greetings to send. I've finished counting what's left of the estate and have the list of debtors for my solicitor. Those messages won't go until long after the Queen has finished. All I can do now is wait.

The breakfast table and my regular stroll are the only activities open to me, and both feel strained and sad on Christmas Day. I try for a table in the corner, but the girl manoeuvres me into my usual spot and pulls the chair out before I have the chance to resist. All my neighbours are there. My silent Americans, staring at their screens; the Japanese family drama; the big group with their daily wasted bread.

There's a commotion in the doorway as the maître de walks in with a bag and a fake white beard. He says 'Ho ho ho' in his thick accent, so that it comes out like a staccato bark. Some of the guests wander over to see if there's anything for them in the sack, always wanting the most from all-inclusivity. The Japanese parents start taking photos, while the American seize the chance to jump back into the buffet queue. No doubt expecting charity on this day of all days, they've left their wallet, phones and handbag on the table.

Nobody is watching me, and this strange, sudden urge bubbles up, like an itch I've been meaning to scratch all day.

I reach over and take the American's phone and then, standing and doing a simple turn on demi-pointe, use the momentum to spin and tap the little Japanese girl's untouched muesli bowl, upending the cereal perfectly into her brother's lap.

Then, it's a simple enough lunge to grab the plate full of croissants with my free hand and return to my seat, tuck the purloined phone under the cushion. I think one of the smaller children sees me, but he's too young to understand, and his Asian counterpart is busy howling, drenched in milk and oats.

My heart is racing as I sit back down, and I have to tell myself to be calm. ('Three years of ballet school training,' I want to say, but have no-one to share it with.)

The Japanese parents rush back and the father shouts at his son, pointing at the mess. I think Mother understands what her boy has been up to, covered as he is in the evidence. She slips a consoling hand onto the daughter's neck.

There's another success on my right, as the Americans are finally forced to speak with each other, he practically begging her to help find the missing device. She reaches over and holds his hand, and I can feel the grin spreading on my face. Father Christmas gives me a look, so I compose myself, return his gaze impassively, and keep on quietly chewing through one croissant, then another, then another.

The response from the Arab family takes longer. Father seems distracted, dealing with crying women in stereo.

Nobody warns you about that aspect of polygyny, my friend. As I crunch through the eighth croissant, I catch the daughter staring at me and I brush crumbs from my lips and offer my sweetest smile. It only lasts a moment, but she seems utterly stricken, as if I had smacked her on the cheek during my pirouette. Maybe, I think, this will help you consider other people.

All in all, it's enough of a victory to propel me through the meetings of the following days. My solicitor, Simon, who I think is going through some sort of personal crisis, seems eager for battle as we work through my list. With one day left in the month, I take the train refreshed, a weight lifted, the ghosts of The Hetton exorcised.

Home again, I catch myself spinning in the living room, smirking at the memory of the fat little boy, the chastened American. Think of Rory's face when my legal notice drops through his door, a terrible start to the new year. I take the spring in my step and apply it to the cleaning, not pausing when I find old papers, not hearing Tony's little homilies in my head. Maybe it's not just the spirit of our old hotel that's gone.

It all comes crashing down that night. I have the television on while I work, and the news is babbling away as I fill another refuse sack. I'm looking at the back wall and thinking about what new colour will work best, when I see a familiar face on the screen.

It's the girl from the Arab family, the striking one in the black cap. She's wearing the same expression she had after our showdown in the breakfast room.

Her father, it seems, was some sort of exile holed up in London. He went to his consulate on Boxing Day to collect some vital document or other, and nobody has seen him since. There are accusations and denials, of course, but the smiling patriarch has vanished into thin air. His daughter is making an appeal.

Perhaps she knew this was coming; perhaps they all did. The little morning ritual was their last free moment together. I saw it, but I didn't understand it.

'You can't tell if your neighbour is in crisis or triumph,' Tony said. I understand that better now. For the next few weeks, there is the lingering taint of guilt at the back of my throat.

It tastes like butter.

THE LEICESTER WRITES SHORT STORY PRIZE 2020

The Queue
MIKI LENTIN

Middle-aged, I was jobless and lacking direction, so I travelled to Athens to volunteer with a charity for a week, cooking for refugees. I wanted to be useful.

You collected me at Oinofyta train station, a coastal town north of Athens, and drove me to the volunteers' house, tapping a cigarette out of a slit in the window of the van. It was Sunday, everything was closed. An 80s classic played on the radio.

My bedroom was in the basement where the food was stored; cans of chickpeas, packets of spices, jars of lentils, boxes of beef tomatoes. There were bars on the window. My room smelt of onions. Condensation trickled down the walls. The tiled floor numbed my bare feet.

It was no longer day, so I made my bed and smoked out of the window. Fully clothed, I rested my head on the lumpy pillow, and tried to fall asleep in my sleeping bag. I left the door ajar and the outside light on. At some stage you clicked it off. I woke in darkness, my forehead cold from a nightmare I could barely piece together. Something about chasing a young girl wearing a red jacket up a hill. Parched, I drank some water straight from the tap in the bathroom, and returned to bed, listening to the dehumidifier dripping in the background.

Friday came quickly. The air was clear, as if it had been cleaned. Feverish, I shivered despite the spring heat. I was helping, I said to myself while washing my hands that morning. Punctured with blisters, I stared at them. The lines and creases seemed more confused than usual, criss-crossing, like webs of dead ends. A nagging sensation of uselessness knotted my stomach. For a week, I'd cooked, scoured pots, cried over onions and served the same people in the same lines waiting for the same food in Oinofyta refugee camp knowing I could leave whenever I wanted, but they'd still be queuing, long after I left.

After we cooked, you asked if I could drive, saying your head was sore from a migraine. I nodded. You threw me the keys.

My temperature rising, I drove erratically, reacting slowly to your warnings of bumps and potholes. You told me we were running late, so I accelerated, and was soon able to read the names of the trucks in front.

At some stage I asked you if the girl with the red furry coat would be there today. She'd been late every day that week, running across the football pitch, wearing trainers with no socks, just as we'd finished packing up. The day before, I'd knocked the saucepan she'd placed upside down on her head, held up two fingers and reminded her, 'two o'clock, tell mama and papa.' She'd run off, crouching down to remove a pebble from her shoe.

'She knows what time to come, they all do,' you said, 'we always come at the same time.'

Couldn't we wait, I wanted to ask, she's just one person, who cares if she's late, but I knew we had a fixed timetable. It was a pointless discussion.

Descending from a hill, Oinofyta refugee camp appeared strewn alongside the main road. Behind a cluster of cypress trees that speared into the sky, I noticed the queue was already thick. The same pregnant woman gripped the wire fence, the flesh of her arms squeezing through the mesh, while a few children dragged sticks around her legs. I slowed onto an unfinished dirt track, and watched hundreds of heads follow the van as we approached the gate.

'I'll do the talking,' you said, rolling down your window.

The security guard appeared tanned from behind my sunglasses. He smoothed his oily widow's peak. You offered him a cigarette straight from the pack and lit it for him. He circled the van, knocking on the driver's window, making me jump. After a few minutes he fidgeted in his leather coat that flapped against his legs, and removed a remote control. Straight-armed, he pointed it at me and laughed, his teeth chipped and yellow, and shouted something in Greek towards the security hut. The gate rattled open, just enough for the van to squeeze through.

'Drive,' you said.

You pointed to the football pitch, 'reverse under that goal.' Plastic bottles and bags lay drowned in a puddle, and above, carpets had been hung and trainers strung from the crossbar of the goalpost, sending slanted shadows onto the penalty box.

The queue magnified in the rear-view mirror as I nudged the van backwards. Lost in the enormity of the queue for a split second, my sweaty hands lost their grip of the steering wheel and hit the horn, emitting a roar. Together, the queue collapsed like a falling wave, hands covering heads, hats and scarves, before emerging one head at a time, gradually coming up for air.

A wind whipped the trees. Aggressive clouds swept down from the mountain. What sun was left burst through, sending streaks of light onto the two lines of the queue, one for men, one for women. Barefoot children tapped saucepans they placed upside down on their heads like space hats, as they danced in and out of the queue, a tempo rising from them.

I felt the eyes of the chattering queue on me as we unpacked the van in tandem. I held the table, you stretched its legs. I unlocked the back door of the van, you lifted the stainless steel pots. I ripped open the bags of flat bread, you piled them one on top of the other. We snapped on latex gloves.

The queue teetered forward like an expectant row of dominoes, breathing as one, chests to backs. Women with chipped nails held open plastic bags and plates, some decorated with ornate flowers, others with hairline cracks. Parallel to the women the men shuffled, their heads bowed, staring into empty, tarnished saucepans and plastic bowls, as if searching for clues.

Who were these people, I thought? What were they doing here? I never asked you why you came. You never asked me.

'How many? Adult, child?' you asked, raising and lowering your hand, before holding up your fingers with the number to me.

My wrist ached from working with the uneven weight of the ladle, doling out one portion of chewy penne smothered with tomato sauce after the other. As I served, I gazed into the distance rather than into their sunken eyes, wanting to be invisible, feeling itchy with having to do this.

'Watch your portion size,' you said, 'it's a long one today.'

You scribbled numbers and notes and arrows in a notepad that was splattered with bits of food. I nodded, as if in code, and shook off some excess food. But the queue noticed, and upped their requests. Six family members became eight, two became four, a child now had a brother, a sister, an aunt.

An hour later the last pot was nearly clean. A gang of young men I hadn't seen before, sporting sharp haircuts and football shirts at the back of the queue strutted forward. They crunched sunflower seeds in their teeth, and spat them onto the ground. One of them was skilfully flicking a football over his head onto the small of his neck, and bending forward while balancing the ball, his arms spread like a bird of prey.

'How many?' you asked the footballer, who ran his fingers through his hair.

'Six,' he laughed, holding a plastic plate while squeezing the back of the neck of his friend. I caught his eye. He shook his head at me. I raised my eyebrows. He pursed his lips together.

'We only have enough for two,' I said, 'I need to keep some for the girl.'

'She's not coming,' you said, 'give him what he wants so we can go.'

'Two,' I looked up at the man.

'Six, come on man,' he said, 'I have wife, boy and girl, mother and father.'

'Two, that's it.' I was immediately shocked at myself for arguing with him.

You shrugged.

Using the ladle I scrapped up two portions and dolloped them onto his plate. As I did, he grasped the handle. Both of us gripping its long neck, he kept his eyes on me, and with his other hand dug out the congealed bits of food that were stuck to the edge of the ladle, and flicked them onto his plate. Still gripping, he licked each finger one at a time, before letting go of the ladle, leaving the metal handle digging into the skin of my palm.

Drops of rain dotted my waterproof jacket.

'Come on, let's go,' you said, looking at the clouds. There was one portion left. You started to pack up. I grabbed a plastic container from the van. I scooped what I could into the box, the food sticking to my fingers through the ripped holes in my latex gloves, stuffing in torn scraps of bread and shreds of parsley and broken penne and tomato sauce. As I squeezed on the lid, sauce seeping from the sides, two fighter jets screamed through the air. I turned my head to follow them over the darkening hills for as long as I could.

'Duck,' you shouted. I didn't react. A football struck me on the side of my head, lurching my neck sideways, as if I was being yanked like a dog by its owner. Split and shattered, my sunglasses fell to the ground, my forehead tingled electrically.

'Fuck,' you said. I looked up. A cheer rose from the men who were now standing around a smoking oil drum at the other end of the football pitch. The footballer chest-pumped one of his friends, waved at me and frisbeed his empty plate against the fence.

'Go fuck yourself,' I muttered in the direction of the men, and dragged hard on a cigarette you held in front of my lips.

The security guard approached, the sun reflecting into my eye from his watch face like a searchlight. He tapped his wrist. 'Closing time,' he grunted.

'Come on,' you said.

'What about the girl?'

'Leave her.'

'She said she'd be here.'

'Forget about her!'

I threw you the keys to the van and ran across the pitch gripping the container of food, my boots spreading dust.

Breathless, my head pounding, blood warming my eye, I sprinted down an alley, tarpaulin covered huts on both sides, ducking under sheets hung on lines blocking my view, coughing through the smoky smell of log fires. I ran deeper into the camp. She had to be here, somewhere. I banged on doors, not waiting for a response. Lights turned on. I shouted something. A few heads poked out. My head spun. My forehead felt like it would burst. My lungs screamed. I ran up a hill. A playground. A few kids were swinging on a tyre roped to a tree. She must be there. I'll give her the food. I'll tap the saucepan on her head. I'll have been useful.

'Get in,' you shouted from the van, screeching to a stop.

I looked around. The kids had dispersed. I slammed the van door, and watched the huts disappear from view as dust blew onto the windows of the van. You turned onto the main road and went through the gears, the container of food warming my lap.

That night you left the light on as I slept. I didn't dream. I was convinced you looked in on me.

The next day you dropped me at the station. My head ached. You hummed along to an indie track I knew on the radio. The air smelled wet. I was very welcome to come again you said. I crouched down to wave goodbye, but you sped off, the van disappearing into the Greek hills.

THE LEICESTER WRITES SHORT STORY PRIZE 2020

Washing Day
KATHERINE HETZEL

The thick burlap wrap in which the Washing Cloths had arrived fell open. Each of the cloths were wrapped separately in more burlap, as was the custom, but the Daughter of Amma's heart stuttered in her chest when she lifted the first cloth free.

Underneath it was something wrapped in a protective layer of black lambswool.

Time stretched, long and thin, as Daughter Tessi carefully laid down the cloth on the table and stared at the alien object. She'd thought her little flock was safe. Had only ever received the lambswool package once, in her first year, *before* she'd had a chance to build relationships in the village.

'Daughter? Are you there?'

Tessi snatched up the object and shoved it into the folds of her skirt where it weighed down her pocket less than it weighed on her conscience. 'Come in, Ailsa.'

The blanket at the door was swept aside.

'Have they come?' Ailsa's eyes shone with excitement.

Tessi forced herself to smile. How well she remembered birthing Ailsa in the depths of winter, pulling her reluctantly from the warmth of her mother's womb, the squalling newborn yelling and raging as only a newborn can against being dragged into the cold. Would Ailsa yell and rage again, fifteen years later, if…?

She gave herself a shake. It might *not* be Ailsa. There were two cloths this time.

'Just arrived.' Tessi pointed and Ailsa skipped across to the table to look.

'Which one's mine?'

Tessi shrugged. 'It doesn't matter. They're both the same,' she lied.

Aisla flung her arms around Tessi and squeezed her tight. 'I'm so excited, Daughter! After my Washing, I shall be Linked!'

Tessi nodded. 'I know.' Gently she pulled away from Aisla's embrace. 'Kody is a good man, Aisla. You will be much blessed, I'm certain.'

How could she even speak these words without them turning to ash and dust in her mouth? She marvelled at her own duplicitousness even as nausea churned her gut like butter. She pressed it down with a hand to her stomach. She had trained for this eventuality, knew she must not give any sign. The Great Amma was depending on her.

Aisla cocked her head to one side. 'Will I still look pretty d'you think, in a plain shift?'

Tessi laughed. Couldn't help it. How like Aisla, to forget that when she did wear the shift, her whole world might be changed in an instant. 'Child, you'd look good in a sack. The Great Amma gave you red hair and green eyes for a reason.'

'She did, didn't she?' Aisla twirled on the spot and then staggered to a stop. 'I must tell Clara!'

She was off then, like a startled hare. Tessi stood at the door, watching the child's long legs flashing under her skirt as she ran to tell her best friend the news. Then she turned slowly back inside. Time to thread her needle.

It took almost no time at all to sew the shifts – they were shapeless things after all, with straight seams along their sides and across the shoulders. Yet hours passed before Tessi completed the task, thanks to the steps necessary to prevent cross-contamination.

Working on only one piece of fabric at a time. Scrubbing the table with natrace. Burning the burlap sacks she spread across her lap to protect her skirts. Melting down the silver needles after every session of sewing, and storing the minute – purified – beads, ready to be resurrected as new needles. Sealing the completed garments in paper wrappings, and writing the recipient's name on them.

The worst part was soaking her hands in the dilute natrace every time she finished handling the fabric. Thank Anuna there were only two shifts to make, because well before the second was finished, Tessi had already scratched at her itching skin until she bled. What must it be like for other Daughters, who received the lambswool-wrapped package and had to make many more shifts for *their* Washing Days?

She tried not to think about which of the two garments she'd sewn was the one.

'Thank you, Daughter,' Clara whispered, taking the parcel from Tessi as though it was something immensely fragile.

'May Great Amma be with you tomorrow.' Tessi turned away.

'Daughter!'

Tessi fought the urge to run, to distance herself from this moment. She'd faced it before of course – the girls all reacted in different ways on receiving their shifts and many of them were understandably nervous. But she'd never had to offer reassurance, knowing what she knew this time. Slowly she turned back. 'Yes, Clara?'

Clara's eyes were bright with tears. 'Do you think…?' She swallowed before continuing. 'Do you think I'll wash clean, Daughter?'

'Only the Great Amma knows, child.'

The words were glib and well-practised, and they hid the truth.

Ailsa received her own parcel with rather more delight, hugging it to her chest and dancing around the yard with her hair flying out behind her like a banner.

'I shall be washed clean and then Linked,' Aisla told Tessi when she finally stopped twirling. 'Clara's going to be my Maid at the Linking, because she doesn't even have a beau yet. We shall both have arta flowers woven into our hair, and we'll wear soft silk slippers for the dancing, and I shall be Kody's breath and he will be mine!'

Tessi couldn't bear it. 'May Great Amma be with you tomorrow,' she muttered, and walked away as quickly as she could without running.

At dawn on Washing Day, Daughter Tessi wrapped herself in a thick wool cloak to ward off the early morning chill. Then she reached into the little nook behind the stove, where she'd hidden the lambswool and its contents. The wool was thrown into the stove, where it smouldered for a moment on the still-warm ashes before bursting into flame and shrivelling to nothing. The glass ampoule it had been protecting went into Tessi's pocket.

The walk to the sacred pool was not a long one, but with every step taken, the weight of responsibility fell heavier on Tessi's shoulders. Finally she reached the pool, and knelt beside it. It was the work of a moment to snap the ampoule open and pour the perfectly clear liquid it contained into the opaque green water.

'Great Amma, choose wisely the next of your Daughters.'

Now all she could do was wait.

It was late afternoon when the Collecting Daughters arrived, the green lines tattooed on both their faces a visible reminder of their special position. They came to every Washing Day of course, but apart from Tessi's first year as this flock's Daughter, they had always gone away empty-handed.

Until now.

This time, their hands would be full.

Washing Days were always a community affair. Everyone from the village came to watch, and afterwards, there would be a feast. A celebration, because Great Amma had blessed the girls and granted them womanhood.

Tessi had no idea how she would manage to eat, afterwards, knowing that only one family would be celebrating.

As sunset approached, Daughter Tessi, now wearing her ceremonial cape – the one embroidered with the symbols of Great Amma and womanhood – walked over the bridge, the excited chatter of the assembled villagers audible even from this distance. The two girls walked beside her, one on either side.

Aisla sighed. 'Our bridge is so ordinary.'

And it was; just rough-hewn stones, carved by a heavy hand and shaped into a simple arch over the stream which fed the pool.

'It does not need to be ornate,' Tessi told her sharply. 'It's symbolic.'

Aisla tossed her hair over her shoulder. 'Because we're crossing into womanhood. I know. But it would've been nice to have a more beautiful one to walk over. What do you think, Clara?'

The day's warmth lingered, but Clara seemed unaware of it; she was shivering when Tessi glanced down at her.

The girl was still nervous, then.

The noise level rose and eager faces turned as Daughter Tessi and her charges walked the last section of path and came to a halt at the pool's side.

Tessi lifted her hand and silence fell.

'Once a girl reaches fifteen years, she is washed,' she said. 'The sacred pools are blessed by Great Amma through her Daughters, so that during the Washing, the water will decide whether the girl is clean and worthy to enter and enjoy the joy of womanhood. If the water decides otherwise, Great Amma gains a new Daughter.' She paused, checking that the Collecting Daughters had taken up their positions beside the pool steps. 'Let the Washing begin. Clara. You will wash first.'

Clara appeared frozen, tear etched deep on her face.

And then Tessi saw it; the bulge in the girl's belly that was so at odds with the rest of her skinny frame, and barely hidden by the loose ceremonial shift. Quick as a flash, she scanned the faces in the crowd. Who–?

There! Sidnay Horith, paler than he'd ever been, guilt writ large across his features. So that was the way of it. There'd have to be a Linking – and fast. But only if…

Suddenly, Aisla reached across and grabbed Clara's hand. 'We've done everything together up to now. Let's wash together, too.' She tugged her friend towards the pool, past the Collecting Daughters, down the steps, and into the murky water.

Tessi's breath caught in her throat as both the red head and the brown disappeared under the green water once, twice, three times. Great Amma, which one would it be? She couldn't bear to watch. She shut her eyes as acid fear burned her stomach. Great Amma, let it only be one… Surely you aren't cruel enough to demand *two* new Daughters from my small flock?

It was the only way to supply Great Amma with Daughters of course; it removed choice. Why would a girl – a woman – voluntarily give up being Linked, and having the chance to bear children? How could a Daughter decide on who to lose from her flock if it was demanded of her? It would be too tempting to protect those she loved and respected; to let go of and lose those she did not favour. No. It was better this way, even if it meant that at least one of the girls she'd watched growing up for the last fifteen years would emerge from the pool bearing a sign so life changing…

She forced her eyes open.

The required number of submersions had been completed. All part of the ceremony, but in reality designed to ensure the various chemicals were thoroughly agitated.

Aisla was first to climb out of the water. She stood, dripping, on the top step.

A wail rose from the crowd, was quickly stifled.

'No,' Aisla whispered, staring at her poisonous green shift. 'No!'

The Collecting Daughters grabbed hold of her before she could run.

All eyes turned toward Clara; her disbelief was obvious as she emerged from the green water, plucking at her own, still-white, garment.

'No!' Aisla screamed. 'She should have the green! Not me! I'm to be Linked! Clara has no man!'

Oh, but she did, she did. And if Clara *had* been the one to emerge wearing the green, she'd have gone from this village, supposedly to become a Daughter of Amma…but Great Amma would never have accepted her. Not now. Not after Sidnay…

'Clara, you are now a woman and blessed by Great Amma.' Tessi had to shout so that she could be heard over Aisla's screams. 'Go, celebrate your future!'

Then she forced herself to look upon the girl whose dreams she had helped to shatter. Would she remember the words required of her at this moment? She hadn't needed to speak them for nigh on twenty years…

'Aisla, Great Amma has chosen you to be one of her Daughters. Go from this place, and set aside your life for her service. May Great Amma protect you.'

Although she failed to protect me when my own Washing Day shift turned the same colour, she added silently, watching as the Collecting Daughters dragged Aisla – still screaming for her mother, for Kody, for a chance to get into the pool and wash again – away.

Great Amma, in whose name fifteen-year old girls were taken from their homes to the temple, to have their hopes of love and husbands and children beaten out of them.

Great Amma, whose initiated Daughters were taught how to sew only one shift at a time because of the chemicals applied to the Washing Cloths.

Great Amma, who caused all her Daughters, once their training was complete, to live in fear of a lambswool-wrapped ampoule arriving with their flock's Washing Cloths.

Great Amma, in whose name women called Daughters acted as unwilling midwives, overseeing the birth of future Daughters.

Great Amma.

A fantasy of maternal care.

THE LEICESTER WRITES SHORT STORY PRIZE 2020

About the Authors

Edward Barnfield is a writer and researcher who was born in Leicester and is currently living in the Middle East. His fiction has appeared in The Short Story, Reflex Fiction, Communicate, GoArchitect and Grindstone Literary Anthology. He was highly commended in the 2019 Manchester Fiction Prize and is currently working on a novel and a collection of short stories. He's on Twitter at: @edbarnfield

Joe Bedford is a writer from Doncaster, UK. His short stories have been published widely, including in *Litro*, *Structo* and *Mechanics' Institute Review* amongst others. His work has won or been placed in the Fish Short Story Prize, the Cambridge Short Story Prize and Waterstones' inaugural Write & Raise prize, and has been Highly Commended for both the Manchester Fiction Prize and Hastings LitFest short story competition. Selections of published stories are available to read on his website. He is currently seeking representation for his novel *A Bad Decade for Good People*.

Judy Birkbeck has short stories in Litro, Lampeter Review, Liars' League, Unthology 9, East of the Web, Aesthetica, Manchester Review, Leicester Writes 2018, Mechanics' Institute Review #15, Ellipsis Zine, The Shadow Booth, the

2019 Dinesh Allirajah short fiction anthology, Lighthouse and Aftermath Magazine, and an essay in Permaculture Magazine. A novel, *Behind the Mask is Nothing*, is published by Holland House Books.

Laura Blake is a writer and magazine editor from Birmingham. She was longlisted for the Edinburgh Flash Fiction Award 2019, the Reflex Winter Flash 2019 and the Retreat West Themed Flash 2019. She was also shortlisted for the Floella Benjamin Trophy 2019.

Born in Sri Lanka, **Tania Brassey** came to London in 1963 to avoid an arranged marriage. But ended up living in a Stately home. She's been an actor, journalist, travel writer and taught singing in the workplace. Her novel about a homeless mother and young daughter in Sri Lanka got a TLC Free Read in 2019. She writes for Children, Short Stories and enjoys Storytelling.

Maureen Cullen lives in Argyll & Bute and has an MA in Creative Writing from Lancaster University. She has been shortlisted in various writing competitions and has had poems and short stories published in magazines and anthologies including Leicester Writes 2017, Northwords Now and The Bristol Prize Anthology 2018. Her current project is a collection of linked short stories based in a fictional town in the West of Scotland. She is a retired social worker.

THE LEICESTER WRITES SHORT STORY PRIZE 2020

Fiona Ennis has a BA in English and Philosophy and an MA in English Literature and Publishing from National University of Ireland, Galway. She also holds a PhD in Philosophy from University College Cork. She lectures in Literature and Philosophy in Waterford Institute of Technology. She won the Molly Keane Creative Writing Award 2019. Her fiction is currently shortlisted for the 2020 Bristol Short Story Prize. Her short stories have also been highly commended in the Manchester Fiction Prize and the Seán Ó Faoláin International Short Story Competition. Her fiction has been published in *Sonder* and is forthcoming in the 2020 Bristol Short Story Prize Anthology. Her poetry has been published in *The Honest Ulsterman*. She has read her work at literary festivals including the Immrama Festival and Waterford Writers' Weekend.

Peter Hankins spent years on commuter trains pecking out a draft novel on his iPad. Since retiring with chronic health problems in the shape of Crohn's disease, he has focused his energy on writing short stories, trying to build up his skills and obtain some much-needed encouragement. His stories have been shortlisted or placed in a number of competitions, including the Alpine Fellowship Prize, the Bridport short story competition, and the Hammond House International Writing Competition. Suitably encouraged, he is now near completing the draft of that full length novel.

THE LEICESTER WRITES SHORT STORY PRIZE 2020

Katherine Hetzel is 'the short author who tells tall tales.' She mostly writes fiction for children, and visits schools to share her love of creative writing with lots of little people.

Granny Rainbow and *More Granny Rainbow* are collections of short stories for younger readers. Katherine's novels are fantasy adventures for middle grade readers but have proven to have a wide crossover appeal. She's been published in several anthologies and was longlisted and published in the *Leicester Writes Short Story Prize Anthology 2017*. She blogs about life and writing at Squidge's Scribbles, runs a small creative writing group called NIBS, and is a volunteer librarian at a local primary school.

Born and brought up in Mansfield, Nottinghamshire, **Richard Hooton** studied English Literature at the University of Wolverhampton before becoming a journalist and communications officer. He has had several short stories published and has been listed in various competitions, including the Cambridge Short Story Prize, Flash 500, Wells Festival of Literature, HE Bates Short Story Competition, Exeter Writers Short Story Competition, Bedford Writing Competition and Ink Tears, as well as winning contests run by Segora, Artificium Magazine, Audio Arcadia and Henshaw Press. He was longlisted in last year's Leicester Writes Short Story Prize with the story "The Edge of Love". Richard lives in Mossley, near Manchester.

THE LEICESTER WRITES SHORT STORY PRIZE 2020

Matt Kendrick is a writer based in the East Midlands, UK. His stories have been published in Bath Flash Fiction, Bending Genres, Craft Literary, Fictive Dream, FlashBack Fiction, Lunate, Spelk, Storgy and elsewhere. He has been listed in various writing competitions and won the Retreat West quarterly flash fiction contest in June 2020. Twitter: @MkenWrites

Farhana Khalique is a writer, editor, voiceover artist and teacher from south-west London. Her writing has appeared in *The Brown Anthology, Reflex Fiction, Lighthouse Literary Journal, Litro, Popshot Quarterly* and elsewhere. Farhana has been longlisted for the Bath Flash Fiction Award, shortlisted for The Asian Writer Short Story Prize, and she has won a Word Factory Apprentice Award. She is also the editor of *Desi Reads*, has been a Reader in Residence for *SmokeLong Quarterly*, and she has performed her work at London's Tara Theatre. Find Farhana @HanaKhalique.

Miki Lentin took up writing while travelling the world with his family a few years ago, and this year was a finalist in the *2020 Irish Writers Centre Novel Fair*. As well as finishing his first book, he writes short stories, the most recent of which achieved second prize in the short memoir competition with *Fish Publishing*. He has achieved second prize in the Momaya Press Short Story Award 2019 and has also been published by @*Villageraw Magazine* and *Elixir*

Magazine online. He also writes book reviews for *MIR Online.* His agent is Cathryn Summerhayes @taffyagent. He also writes books reviews for MIR Online and has appeared three times at MIR Live.

Dan Powell is a prize-winning author of short fiction and First Story Writer-in-Residence. His debut collection of stories, *Looking Out of Broken Windows*, was shortlisted for the Scott Prize and longlisted for the Frank O'Connor International Short Story Award and the Edge Hill Prize. He is currently working on his PhD as a Doctoral Researcher in Creative Writing at University of Leicester. His research explores preclosure and closural staging in short fiction. Dan can be found online as @danpowfiction.

Radhika Praveen grew up in Mumbai, feeding on *Amar Chitra Katha* picture books, and the *Time, Discover* and *Life* magazines that she always found in her father's briefcase. She survived a jargon-intense career as a content editor at various IT publications by venting out her thoughts on her website where she still occasionally blogs. She has recently been awarded a Doctorate in Creative Writing, the subject of which was a novel in the historical fiction genre. She lives in Milton Keynes with her husband and two boys, and insists that no neighbours were harmed during the writing of 'Sarika and Me'.

THE LEICESTER WRITES SHORT STORY PRIZE 2020

Claire Sheret has recently taken up creative writing after a twenty year career in Journalism and Public Relations. 'Swimming Against the Tide' is her first submission to a short story competition.

Harjit Keanu Singh is a 22 year old Black Asian author from Northampton. His urban fantasy book, *SEMIAUTOMAGIC was published in* 2018. He graduated from De Montfort University shortly after with a BA in Creative Writing and Journalism. Harjit has since gone on to pursue an MA in Creative Writing from De Montfort University. Harjit writes stories which explore representation, mental health, sexuality and social inequality. His current project is his novella, psychological thriller BLOOM. He hopes to write an acclaimed bestseller one day.

Originally from Cheshire, **John McMenemie** studied architecture before relocating to London to pursue a career in music. He still draws buildings and still writes songs, but focuses mainly on writing fiction. John's work has appeared in Sovereign Magazine and The Cabinet of Heed, and been long-listed for the Sandstone Press 2020 short fiction competition. He splits his days between North London with his partner and daughter, and a time bubble on Pluto with his pet dinosaur brain and a fairly useless robot called Alan. Follow him on Twitter @cheshire_cactus

Alison Woodhouse is a teacher and writer. She has won and been placed in many competition and is widely published, both online and in print. Her debut Novella in Flash will be published by AdHoc Fiction later this year. She has an MA in Creative Writing from Bath Spa and is one of the team who organise the Bath Short Story Award.

Judith Wilson is a London-based writer and journalist. She graduated with Distinction from the MA in Creative Writing at Royal Holloway, University of London, in 2019. She won 1st Prize for the London Short Story Prize 2019, 1st Prize for the Lorian Hemingway Short Story Competition 2017 and 3rd Prize for the Brick Lane Bookshop Short Story Prize 2019. She was also shortlisted for the London Short Story Prize 2018. Judith is completing her first novel, set in London in the 1860s. Find her @judithwrites.

THE LEICESTER WRITES SHORT STORY PRIZE 2020

Judging Panel

Rebecca Burns is a writer of short stories and fiction. Her work has been published in over thirty online and print journals. She has won or been placed in many competitions including the Fowey Festival of Words and Music Short Story Competition. Her debut collection of short stories, *Catching the Barrmundi*, was published by Odyssey Books in 2012 and was longlisted for the Edge Hill Award. Her second collection, *The Settling Earth* (2014) was also longlisted for the Edge Hill. Her debut novel, *The Bishop's Girl*, was published in 2016, and her third collection of short stories, *Artefacts and Other Stories*, appeared in 2017, both again published by Odyssey Books. Her second novel, *Beyond the Bay* was published in September 2018.

Selma Carvalho is a British-Asian writer and author of three non-fiction works documenting the Goan presence in colonial East Africa. She headed the 'Oral Histories of British-Goans Project' archived at the British Library. Her short fiction and poetry have been published in various journals and anthologies, among them by Kingston University Press and Parthian Books. She has received a nod from over 35 literary competitions including Fish, Bath, London Short Story, and as winner of the Leicester Writes Short Story Prize. Her collection of short stories was longlisted for the SI Leeds Literary Prize. Her novella titled, *Sisterhood of Swans* is forthcoming by Speaking Tiger, India.

Mark Newman has been shortlisted for the Costa Short Story Award, highly commended in the New Writer Prose & Poetry Awards and Bristol Prize longlisted. His work has won competitions judged by Alison Moore, Tania Hershman and David Gaffney. He has been published in *Firewords Quarterly*, *Fiction Desk* and *Paper Swans*. He has eight stories in the Retreat West competition anthology *Inside These Tangles, Beauty Lies* and his debut short story collection *My Fence is Electric & Other Stories* was published by Odyssey Books in February 2020.